What Readers Are Saying about Forbidden Doors

"Nothing I have seen provides better spiritual equipment for today's youth to fight and win the spiritual battle raging around them than Bill Myers's Forbidden Doors series. Every Christian family should have the whole set."

> C. Peter Wagner
> President, Global Harvest Ministries

"During the past 18 years as my husband and I have been involved in youth ministry, we have seen a definite need for these books. Bill fills the need with comedy, romance, action, and riveting suspense with clear teaching. It's a nonstop page-turner!"

> Robin Jones Gunn
> Author, Christy Miller series

"Bill Myers's books will help equip families. It's interesting, too, that the Sunday school curriculum market, for which I write, is examining topics such as reincarnation and out-of-body experiences. The Forbidden Doors books are timely."

> Carla Williams
> Mother and freelance writer

"Fast-moving, exciting, and loaded with straightforward answers to tough questions."

> Jon Henderson
> Author

The Ancients

BILL MYERS

Tyndale House Publishers, Inc. Wheaton, Illinois

Visit Tyndale's exciting Web site at www.tyndale.com

Published in association with the literary agency of Alive
Communications, Inc., 1465 Kelly Johnson Blvd., Suite 320,
Colorado Springs, CO 80920.

Scripture quotations are taken from the *Holy Bible,* New
Living Translation, copyright © 1996. Used by permission of
Tyndale House Publishers, Inc., Wheaton, Illinois 60189. All
rights reserved.

ISBN 0-8423-5971-0

Printed in the United States of America

02   01   00   99   98
7   6   5   4   3   2   1

To David Spargur, longtime friend and musical partner

In the last times some will turn away from what we believe; they will follow lying spirits and teachings that come from demons.

1 Timothy 4:1

1

The eagle soared through the clear blue sky. Sleek and beautiful, it rose higher and higher. Suddenly it dipped and dove, screaming through the air like a jet fighter.

Rebecca Williams watched in delight as the wonderful creature swooped low toward the ground. Then, at the last second, it pulled up and sailed high into the sky in a graceful arc.

And what a sky. Rebecca's delight changed to wonder as she saw that the sky had taken on a dark, purplish hue. But what really mesmerized her was the weird geometric pattern covering the sky: lines, triangles, and squares were arranged in a swirling, concentric pattern that made them impossible to distinguish from one another. And yet the pattern was strong and focused, making an instant imprint on her mind.

The eagle's harsh cry rang out across the horizon, distracting Rebecca from the pattern in the sky.

"Rebecca! Be careful!"

She turned to see Ryan Riordan shouting and running toward her. She looked back at the eagle. Now it was diving toward her. She threw her hands in front of her face and darted to the left. But the eagle did not follow. It swooshed past her, heading directly for Ryan.

She turned and saw Ryan's mouth open. He lifted his hand to protect his face. He began to scream, but it was too late. The sharp, leathery talons slashed at his neck and—

"Noooo!" Rebecca woke up with a start.

Her face was damp with sweat, and she was breathing hard.

Before she could get her bearings she heard, "Will you stop all that whimpering?"

She spun around to see Scotty, her younger brother. She was about to yell at him for being in her room when she realized that she wasn't in her room at all. In fact, she wasn't even in her house. She had been napping on a plane.

A plane heading for New Mexico.

"Honey, are you all right?" Mom looked at her from the seat next to Scotty's, her face showing concern.

"I'm OK," Becka said, wiping the perspiration from her forehead. "I just had . . . It was only a dream."

"Must have been pretty weird," Scott said. "You were making all kinds of noise."

"It was an eagle," Rebecca explained. "A huge one. It flew right at me and then wound up attacking Ryan."

Scott held her gaze a moment. There was no missing the trace of concern in his eyes. This had happened before. Her dreams. Usually they were some sort of omen. Finally he shrugged. "You're just worried about the trip."

She could tell he was trying to reassure her. She nodded. "Yeah. It's just . . ."

He glanced back at her. "Just what?"

"This whole assignment." She hesitated, then continued, "Doesn't it seem a little stranger than the others?"

Scott gave a half smirk. "Stranger than fighting voodoo in Louisiana?"

Becka said nothing.

"Or tracking down make-believe vampires in Transylvania? Or facing down demons in Los Angeles?"

Rebecca took a deep breath. OK, so he had a point. Life had become pretty incredible. Still . . .

"What are you guys talking about?" It was Ryan, Rebecca's sort-of boyfriend. He had turned around from the seat ahead of them and was grinning.

Becka felt a wave of relief. She knew she'd been dreaming, but it was still good to see him and know he was all right. Come to think of it, it was always good to see Ryan Riordan. If not because of their special friendship, then because of the gentle warmth she always felt inside when they were together.

"We were talking about this trip," Scott said. "Becka's afraid this one is stranger than the others."

Ryan's smile faded. "What makes you say that?"

"I don't know." She shrugged. "Just a feeling I guess."

"At least we get to stay in a fancy hotel again," Scott said. "What's it called? The Western Ground on the Cliff?" He leaned back, folding his hands behind his head. "Sounds pretty hoity-toity to me. Like one of those expensive, something-on-the-something hotels in Beverly Hills."

"I'm just glad to be going this time," Ryan said. "I went bananas when you guys were in L.A."

Rebecca nodded. She was glad he was with them, too.

"Well, Becka's right about one thing," Scott admitted. "Something's definitely up. Z never sends us out on boring assignments, that's for sure."

Becka and Ryan both nodded in agreement. Z was their friend from the Internet. He'd sent them to help folks all over the world. And yet, to this day, Scott and Rebecca had no idea who Z really was. Not that they hadn't tried to find out . . . but somehow, someway, their attempts had always met with failure. Z's identity remained a mystery.

"Actually," Ryan said with a grin, "I'm pretty excited to be visiting an Indian tribe. I mean, I've always liked reading about Native

American culture. I think they are a noble people who got a raw deal."

Rebecca nodded. "Taking their land was a wrong that we'll never fully repay. Kinda like slavery. And you're right about their culture. They've got a real respect for nature that we could all learn from."

"I suppose," Scott said. "But aren't some tribes really involved in weird spiritual stuff? You know, like shamanism and séances and visions?"

Ryan nodded slowly. "But some of that is in the Bible."

"So?" Scott asked.

"So they must have some truth to them."

"There's some truth in everything," Scott countered. "That's the devil's favorite trick . . . a little truth, a lotta lie."

Before Ryan could answer, Becka called out, "Wow! Look down at that canyon!"

Mom and Scott crowded in close to her so they could see out the window. There, below them, was a beautiful canyon, its cliff walls shimmering red, yellow, and purple in the sunset.

The captain's voice came over the loud-speaker. "Well, folks, we're beginning our descent into Albuquerque. Please fasten your seat belts. We should be on the ground in just a few minutes."

On the ground far below the plane, an Indian brave was running through the desert. Above him, the huge canyon walls towered and rose toward the sky. Beside him, a river flowed, its power thundering and cutting into the rock and sandstone.

The brave's name was Swift Arrow. He ran because he wanted to crest the hill at the far end of the canyon in time to see the sunset. As he neared the top, he could see the bright yellow sun dipping behind the mountain ahead. When he arrived, he raised his hands to the sky and called, "Father, you are the master creator. I praise you for the beauty you have made."

Far in the distance, a rumble caught his attention. He turned and looked behind him. Dark clouds were beginning to gather. A storm was brewing. Suddenly a great lightning bolt cut through the sky, and then another, and another. Jagged lines seemed to fill the sky, forming triangles and squares, all arranged in a swirling, concentric pattern. . . .

Swift Arrow stared as the light from the bolts faded, his heart beginning to pound in fear. He'd seen that sign in the sky before. He lowered his head and began to pray. "Lord, deliver my people from their bondage. Free them from the snares of a thousand years. Help them to see beyond the old legends, the old fears, the ancient beliefs. Help them see your truth."

He was startled by another burst of light and raised his head just in time to see the remainder of another lightning bolt slice through the sky.

Swift Arrow grimaced as a mixture of fear and concern swept over him.

~

Rebecca lurched forward in her seat as the Jeep roared across the bumpy desert road. It had been nearly three hours since they'd boarded the vehicle at the Albuquerque airport. And judging by the bruises she was accumulating and the perpetual look of discomfort on Mom's face in the front seat, it was about two hours and fifty-nine minutes too long.

Of course, Scotty and Ryan enjoyed every bone-jarring bounce and buck. They were busy having a great time. All around were beautiful red rock formations rising high into the bright blue sky. To the left of the vehicle, three colossal boulders, each about three stories high, balanced on top of each other. To their right, a five-hundred-foot butte jutted upward, its smooth, flat top a stark contrast to its jagged sides. In the distance rose a vast range of peaks. Their driver was pointing to those peaks, saying, "The village is in the middle of that mountain range. I can drive you most of the way up, but you'll have to go the last few miles on foot. No one can reach Starved Rock by car or truck."

"You want us to climb those peaks?" Scott asked in alarm. "Are you kidding?"

The driver laughed. "It's not that hard, boy. And it won't take you too long. Come Saturday, I'll be waiting at the drop-off point to pick you up. Noon sound all right?"

Mom nodded. "That should give us enough time to make our flight, Mr. Doakey."

The driver grinned. "Just call me Oakie. Everyone else does."

"Oakie?" Scott asked.

"Sure, when your last name is Doakey, what else would you expect?"

"Oakie Doakey?" Scott laughed. "That's good." He threw Ryan a look, but Ryan didn't seem to notice.

Rebecca frowned. Ryan had spent most of the ride in silence, his attention focused on the scenery. When he had spoken, it was in a soft and reverent voice—almost as though he were inside a huge church. Granted, he seemed peaceful and relaxed. But he also seemed preoccupied—as if he wasn't entirely there. Rebecca wasn't sure why this made her uncomfortable. Maybe it was just jealousy. After all, she was used to being the focus of much of Ryan's attention. But deep inside, she knew that wasn't it. There was something else bothering her. . . .

She couldn't put her finger on it, but she could swear something was happening. Something . . . unnatural. Try as she might, she couldn't stop the feeling from rising up inside her. Something was wrong.

They'd been in New Mexico for only a few hours, but already she knew something was very wrong.

2

An hour later, Oakie Doakey pulled the Jeep to a stop near the base of a steep hill. For some time now the road had grown steeper, and now it dead-ended into a wall of sheer rock.

"This is as far as I can take you," he said. "Just over that hill is a footbridge that connects you to the next cliff. Once you cross to the other side, you just keep heading up the same direction through the hills and you'll hit the village of Starved Rock before you know it. But I'd hurry. Looks like a storm is coming."

All four of them turned in the direction Oakie was looking. An awesome thunderhead was building in the west.

"We'd better get going," Mom said as she hoisted a small suitcase out of the back of the Jeep.

"I'm glad we packed light," Rebecca said as she grabbed her makeup kit and another small bag.

Ryan lifted his backpack out of the Jeep, while Scott grabbed the laptop computer and a few other odds and ends.

Mom paused and turned back to Oakie. "Excuse me, but did you say something about a footbridge?"

Oakie nodded. "That's right. It's a rope bridge. You'll find them once in a while in these back areas. The Indians use them to get around the cliffs."

Becka and Mom glanced at each other. The words *rope bridge* and *cliff* did not sound encouraging. Finally Mom cleared her throat, but Becka noted that her voice sounded a little thinner and just a little higher than before when she said, "I presume they are safe?"

Oakie flashed her a grin. "Just take one step at a time and you'll be fine."

"I see." Mom nodded, though it was obvious she was anything but reassured. "Well, thank you for your help, Mr. Doakey . . . and for the advice."

Oakie nodded, then dropped the Jeep into gear and turned it around. "See you all on Saturday!" he shouted. "And good luck."

Becka wasn't sure, but it almost sounded like he was laughing as he started back down the steep road. Suddenly she felt a sense of abandonment. Here they were, out in the wilderness, completely on their own. Well, not completely. She knew God was with them. He always was. Still . . .

She took a deep breath to calm herself. It wouldn't have been so bad if the sky weren't growing darker and far more ominous with each passing minute.

"We'd better get moving," Mom said, and they were off. The climb was steep but not impossible. As the storm cloud continued to build in front of them, it eventually cast its shadow over them. The coolness was a welcome relief from the heat. . . . Rebecca figured it had dropped from 105 to 95 degrees. Not exactly a cold snap, but it did feel better.

Then there was the darkness. Becka was grateful for the shade and its coolness, but there was something eerie about that darkness. She didn't like it . . . not one bit.

They had been climbing for nearly half an hour when they finally saw it. The hanging bridge. From a distance it looked like a slender thread suspended between two mountains.

"Think that will hold us?" Ryan asked.

"I don't know," Scott said. "From here it looks like a piece of dental floss."

"At least dental floss is hard to break," Rebecca said. "That bridge looks more like it's made from cobwebs."

"Now, kids," Mom said. She was trying to be encouraging, but it was obvious she was as much on the nervous side as they were. "I'm sure when we get there we'll see that it will hold us just fine."

Rebecca wished Mom had sounded more convincing . . . but that was hard to do when you weren't convinced. And she knew Mom wasn't.

They continued to approach the bridge. Fortunately, the closer they got, the better it looked. The rope was heavy and well constructed. There were, however, two small problems. . . .

The first was that you could see through

the bridge. The rope was heavily knotted
and formed squares that were eighteen
inches on each side. But while it was easy
enough to walk on, it was also easy enough
to see through. All the way to the ground.
Five hundred feet below.

"Just don't look down," Scotty suggested.

"We've *got* to look down," Becka complained. "We have to make sure we step on a
piece of rope and not a piece of sky."

Ryan nodded but added, "As long as we
hold on to the sides, we'll be OK."

Becka studied the bridge. He was right.
There was a thick rope on each side to hold
on to. The only problem was that the rope
moved, right along with the bridge. Which
brought them to the second problem. . . .
Everything moved. Constantly. Even a slight
breeze caused the entire bridge to swing and
sway.

For a long moment, everyone stood and
stared. Finally Ryan cleared his throat. "I'll,
uh, I'll go first." He adjusted his backpack in
preparation. Then he turned to Mom. "You
want me to take your suitcase? I've got a free
hand."

Mom hesitated, but Becka knew she was
aware that hanging on to the suitcase and
hanging on to the rope could be a problem.

"Well, I—" She looked at Ryan, concerned. "Are you sure you'll be all right?"

"No problem." Ryan took the bag from her and started out onto the bridge. Immediately it began to sway.

"Be careful," Rebecca called, although she was sure he would be. Who wouldn't be careful with a five-hundred-foot drop staring you in the face?

The bridge was only a hundred feet across, but by the time Ryan got to the middle, it was swaying pretty hard. Still, after another minute or two, he had managed to cross it safely.

"I'll go next," Scott said as he grabbed the computer.

The bridge seemed to sway even more as Scott eased his way across, but, like Ryan, he made it across without much of a problem.

Mom went next. A little more slowly, a little more carefully, but finally, she also made it to the other side.

Now it was Rebecca's turn.

"Hurry, Beck!" Scott called. "That thundercloud is getting a lot closer."

Becka glanced up. It was true. The cloud hovered directly overhead, and it seemed to be drawing lower and closer. She took a deep breath, wrapped the handle of the makeup bag around her wrist, and stepped out.

Instantly, the bridge swayed under her

weight. It was scary but nothing she couldn't handle. She gripped the side ropes fiercely and took two more steps. Then another, another, and another. Except for the slight dizziness she felt when she glanced down (a five-hundred-foot drop will do that to a person), she was doing just fine.

Until the wind came.

Although they had all been watching the thundercloud approach, no one had expected the wind to kick up so fast. Or so hard.

Almost instantly the bridge began to sway. Violently.

Becka let out a scream and froze. She didn't dare move her feet. It was all she could do to keep her balance when she stood still, let alone when she walked.

"Come on, Beck!" Scott shouted. "Keep coming!"

But Rebecca could not. She would not. She could barely move at all.

The wind grew stronger, and the bridge swayed harder. It arced out a full ten feet to the left and then swung back a full twelve feet to the right. The arc grew with each swing, and Becka found it more and more difficult to hang on.

"Hold on!" Mom screamed. Then, turning

to the boys, she shouted, "She's losing her grip!"

Despite the heat of the day, Rebecca was cold with terror. She swung to the left fifteen feet, then to the right almost twenty. Things were getting worse as she kept swinging back and forth, farther and farther.

It was on the fourth or fifth swing that she lost her footing. Her left foot shot through the gap in the ropes, and she went down.

She screamed as she fell—until her right leg snagged in the rope.

The bridge swayed back to the left. Rebecca's weight pushed hard against the ropes, and they spread farther apart. As they spread, Rebecca slipped farther through the gap.

Now the bridge was swaying to the right. As it did, Rebecca's body slipped the rest of the way through the gap. Fortunately her leg was still caught in the ropes, but that meant she was hanging, dangling over the gorge by a single leg.

"Becka!" Ryan shouted. "Beck, hang on!"

She lunged for the nearest rope rail but failed, unable to grab it. The bridge swayed back to the right—and her leg slipped.

Mom saw it and screamed. Becka saw her mom start toward the bridge, but Ryan and Scotty grabbed her arm.

"No!" Ryan shouted. "You can't go out

there. The extra weight on the bridge will only make things worse."

Scott turned to Becka and yelled, "Grab the rail! You can do it!"

There were only seconds to spare. Becka's leg was loosening, and she would fall. She lunged for the rope again.

And missed again.

Her leg slipped a bit more. She tried again, but the farther she reached, the more her leg slipped. Realizing that her makeup bag hampered her reach, she let it go, watching for a brief, dizzying second as it tumbled toward the desert floor.

She had time for one more try. If she missed, her fate would be the same as the makeup bag's.

The bridge started back to the left.

"Please, Jesus!" she gasped. "Help me. . . . Help me. . . ." Rebecca stretched for all she was worth—but her leg pulled free, and she began to fall. She screamed, her arms waving and flaying . . . until she caught hold of something. One last strand of rope.

But would it hold? More important, could she pull herself back up onto the bridge? But as the bridge reached the arc of its swing and began falling in the other direction, the force helped lift her. She took advantage of the movement and with one hard tug found herself lying back on the bridge, gripping its sides with both hands as it swayed back and forth, back and forth.

She was safe.

"Thank you, Jesus. Thank you. . . ."

She heard commotion at the end of the bridge. Scott was shouting about going out and saving her.

"Just stay there!" she yelled. "I'm all right! Just stay there till the wind dies down!"

Slowly the wind began to ease. The swaying grew less and less. When Becka was finally sure it was safe to stand again, she rose to her feet. And then, with the encouragement of the others, she slowly finished crossing the bridge.

When she arrived, she fell into Ryan's arms, trying to hold back her tears, to catch her breath. As Ryan held her, and as Mom and Scotty asked again and again if she was OK, Becka slowly raised her eyes from the bridge—up toward the nearest peak. She wasn't sure why she looked up, but she immediately wished she hadn't.

It was there for only an instant. Then it was gone. But she was certain she'd seen it. The outline of a man, silhouetted against the setting sun. . . .

A man with two great horns rising from his skull.

3

Things were less
dangerous once they crossed the bridge, but
they weren't any easier. The heat grew more
and more oppressive until it was nearly
unbearable, which only made their climb
over rocks and rugged terrain that much
more difficult. Rain would have been a welcome, cooling relief. But though the storm

continued to flash its lightning and boom with thunder, not a drop fell.

Within half an hour the ground had leveled off. The straggling group had reached the top of the plateau. Now all they had to do was cross to the village, which Oakie Doakie had said was nestled in the hills up ahead.

Although there was no rain, the wind kicked up again. It whipped and howled through the surrounding hills, making a mournful, wailing cry. Becka thought it sounded almost human.

Awwooo . . .

Rebecca and Scott glanced at each other uncomfortably.

"Was that my imagination, or did the wind just say, 'Yoouuu'?" Scott asked.

Rebecca tried to shrug it off. "It's just the wind."

Awwooo . . .

"See?" she said, doing her best to sound cheerful. "Same as before. It's just the wind."

Scaaah . . .

"Did you hear that?" Scott exclaimed. "It called my name!"

"No, it didn't. It said, 'Scaaah.'"

"So I should feel better because it can't spell?" he quipped.

Rebecca laughed in spite of herself.

"Hey, guys," Ryan called from up ahead. "I think I see the village."

Scott, Becka, and Mom hurried to catch up with him. Now they could see it too. Rows and rows of crude shacks and small sod huts peeked out from behind a distant hill.

"That must be it," Mom said.

"Yeah," Scott agreed. "Only where's our hotel?"

"It's probably at the other end of the village," Ryan suggested. "That looks like the older part of the village. All the new stuff must be at the other end, behind that ridge."

They walked for nearly an hour. As they came closer and closer to the village, Ryan's gaze seldom left the huts. "This is so cool," he said. "It's just like I imagined. Just like the history books. It's like we've been dropped back in time."

"Yeah, great," Scotty replied. "Only where's our hotel? We should be able to see it by now."

At last they reached the edge of the village and entered. A young Indian woman carrying a baby came out of a nearby hut and watched them. They waved self-consciously, and she nodded—but she said nothing.

Farther on, an old man, his long white hair divided into two braids, approached them. When he came within ten feet of them, he simply stopped and continued to stare.

"Hello, there," Ryan ventured. He gave a slight wave to the old man. But the man barely acknowledged his presence.

Ryan shrugged and looked around. Becka followed his gaze and spotted a younger man—she guessed he was around twenty—lugging a large bag of grain over his shoulder.

"Excuse me," Ryan called. "Would you help us out?"

The man turned and stopped. He studied Ryan suspiciously.

"Do you speak English?" Ryan asked.

"Of course. Everyone speaks English."

"Great," Ryan said. "We're looking for a man named Swift Arrow. We have something to—"

The Indian cut him off. "He's not here. He's gone on a walkabout."

"A what?" Ryan asked.

"A walkabout."

"I don't understand. . . ."

"It's like a meditation. A man goes into the desert to think and pray."

"Ah."

"He should be back tomorrow."

"OK," Ryan answered politely. "A walkabout, eh? That's an Indian term I wasn't familiar with."

"It's not Indian," the man replied. "It's Australian. Didn't you see *Crocodile Dundee?*"

"What?"

"It's a movie."

"Oh . . . well, yes, of course."

"You can rent it down at my video store if you're interested."

"You have a video store?" Scott asked in surprise.

"We pack in all the latest movies."

"Do you guys have computers?"

The young man gave him a puzzled look and then broke into a grin. Suddenly he raised his arm and, in a stiff, melodramatic fashion, answered, "Yes . . . we sell 'um many buffalo hides to buy magic screen that glow in dark."

"Pardon me?"

"Glowing screen, heap big magic. Help me speak to spirits on Internet. Impress many squaws."

Becka bit her lip to keep from laughing. Ryan's expression showed he felt foolish enough without her adding to his humiliation. "Oh, I get it," he said with a slow, self-deprecating grin. "Just because the village looks like it's out of the history books doesn't mean the people are."

The young man shrugged good-naturedly. "I know it's hard to believe, but we're as ready for the twenty-first century as anyone." He returned Ryan's smile and turned to leave. "See you around, dude."

"Wait! Excuse me," Rebecca called.

The man turned back again.

"Would you tell us where our hotel is . . . the, uh . . ." She turned to Mom. "What is it called?"

"The Western Ground on the Cliff," Mom said.

The young man look puzzled, then broke into another grin. "The Western Ground on the Cliff is over there. Just past that row of homes to your left. You can't miss it."

"Thanks!" Rebecca said.

"Don't mention it," the man said with a chuckle and then moved off.

The group headed in the direction the Indian had indicated. And sure enough, as soon as they had passed the row of huts, they came to a sign that read The Western Ground on the Cliff. But there was no hotel in sight. Only the sign, which was made up of white paint scrawled on some faded, wooden planks.

"I don't get it," Scott said. "Where's the hotel?"

"You must be the Williams party."

They turned to see a boy of eleven or twelve approaching them from a nearby hut.

"That's—that's not the hotel, is it?" Rebecca pointed toward the hut with a worried look.

The boy laughed. "Nah, that's just where my family and I live."

Rebecca breathed a sigh of relief.

"So could you tell us exactly where the hotel is?" Mom asked.

The boy smiled again. "There is no hotel, ma'am. This is a campground."

Rebecca and Scott looked at each other. Then at Ryan. Then at Mom. No one looked terribly happy.

The boy continued, "Your friend has reserved two of our best campsites for you. He also purchased two tents, four sleeping bags, and a week's worth of supplies."

For a long moment there was nothing but silence. Finally Scott began shaking his head and mumbling, "Good ole Z . . ."

"Well, at least we have sleeping bags," Mom said with what was clearly forced cheerfulness. "Let's make the most of it, shall we? You boys can have one tent, and we girls will take the other."

"Wonderful," Scott continued to mutter. "Just wonderful."

Becka echoed her brother's lack of enthu-
siasm.

But not Ryan. He actually seemed excited.
"I think it's great," he said. "I wouldn't feel
right staying in a fancy hotel here anyway.
This is like an adventure."

"We'll see how adventurous you feel after
a night on this hard ground," Scott grumbled as he kicked the rocky soil.

Ryan didn't seem to even hear him.

"You'd better start setting up your tents,"
the Indian boy said. "It's going to be dark
soon."

~

A few hours later, Rebecca leaned against
Ryan's shoulder. The group was sitting
around the fire, cooking hot dogs and
baked beans. It wasn't as elegant as room ser-
vice in some fancy hotel, but it was definitely
more romantic, and Becka loved it. She
would have loved it even more if Ryan had
paid some attention to her.

It wasn't that he ignored her, but she definitely got the feeling she came in second
when compared to the sights and sounds
around them: the mountains, the desert
night sky, and all of the Indian culture. Well—
Becka glanced around them—who could

blame him? How could anyone compete with such majestic beauty?

When they finally crawled into their tents, Becka was surprised at how much the ordeal at the bridge had taken out of her. Despite the hard ground, when she slid into her sleeping bag, she was asleep within seconds.

The next morning she woke up to the sound of a hawk screeching overhead. For the briefest second she remembered her dream on the airplane. But the memory quickly faded in the peace and tranquillity of early morning in Starved Rock. Though she heard Scott and Ryan scurrying about making breakfast—most likely cold cereal and milk—she gave a long stretch and decided to stay with Mom a bit longer in the tent. Something about the chilly morning, the warm tent, and the complete and utter peace Becka felt made it more than a little difficult to rise and get moving.

~

After breakfast Scott and Ryan decided they'd explore the village a bit. Last night when they had arrived, it was nearly dark, and they really hadn't seen much. So now they were ready to go.

They spotted the Indian boy who ran the

campground and asked him what there was to see.

The boy smiled. "Not much, I'll tell you that. But if you want the grand tour, I'll take you."

"Great," Scott said. "But don't you have to check in people coming to the camp?"

The boy smiled sadly. "Nobody comes to this camp. Not anymore."

Scott and Ryan exchanged glances.

"My name is Little Creek," the boy said, extending his hand.

"Hi, Little Creek." Ryan reached out and shook his hand. "My name is Ryan."

"And I'm Scott Williams," Scott added, also shaking Little Creek's hand.

"I'm very glad you have come to visit," Little Creek said. "We used to get tourists but not for several months now . . . not since the drought. Come on, I'll show you the sights." With that, he turned and started down the road. Scott and Ryan fell in step beside him.

"How long has the drought been going on?" Scott asked.

"It started during the last growing season, killing most of last year's crop."

Ryan scowled. "I'm sorry to hear that."

Little Creek nodded. "And it's continued

into this year. Many people didn't even plant this spring because the soil is so dry."

"Can't you irrigate or something?" Scott asked. "I mean, isn't that what modern farmers do?"

"*Wealthy* modern farmers, sure. But it costs too much to run irrigation pipes all the way up into these mountains."

"That's not a great situation," Ryan said.

Little Creek nodded. "Our people have always depended on the rain. The crops we grow don't need much, but there has been no rain for so long that many people are thinking of leaving the village and moving."

Scott glanced about as they moved past the small shacks and sod huts. "Why don't you just pack up the whole village?" he asked. "Doesn't seem like it would be too hard. There's not that much stuff."

Little Creek smiled. "Things are easy to pack, but people aren't. Our traditions weigh much more than our material goods. And they are a much heavier load."

"What's that supposed to mean?" Ryan asked.

Little Creek smiled. "It means the old people are too stubborn to move."

Soon the three came to the end of the village. Just beyond it was a huge rock, bigger than any boulder Scott or Ryan had ever seen.

"Check it out," Scott said, pointing to the colossal rock. It jutted up against the sky like a gnarled, clenched fist.

"That's Starved Rock," Little Creek explained. "That's where the village gets its name."

"Why do they call it that?" Ryan asked as they moved closer to examine the big boulder.

"Back in the 1880s, a hundred braves made their last stand in this place. They were surrounded by cavalry, but instead of the soldiers coming up the mountain and fighting like men, they merely stopped the braves from escaping . . . until each and every one had died of starvation."

"That's awful," Ryan said.

Little Creek nodded. "It is said that their spirits still cry out from these rocks at night."

"No kidding?" Scott asked.

"It's all very sad," Ryan said, shaking his head.

Little Creek hesitated a moment, then shrugged. "All Indian stories are sad. I learned early not to ask my grandfather the meanings of the names and locations of things. There were always sad stories behind them."

"If you didn't ask your grandfather, then how did you learn them?" Ryan asked.

Little Creek laughed. "Grandfather told me, whether I asked or not. We Indians are very big on oral history, you know. It's another one of our traditions."

"So what about these spirits that are supposed to cry out at night?" Scott asked. "Have you ever heard them?"

Again Little Creek shrugged. "Yes and no. It could just be the wind. No one is certain. Dark Bear claims that they are spirit voices. He also claims that he is the only one who knows what they are saying."

Scott and Ryan exchanged looks. They both remembered the eerie sounds they had heard in the wind on their way up to the village.

"Who's Dark Bear?" Scott asked.

For a moment Little Creek said nothing; then he took a deep breath and answered, "He's the tribal shaman, a very powerful medicine man. I don't know if you guys believe in that kind of thing, but . . . Dark Bear is the one person you should avoid contact with in our village."

"Why?" Scott asked.

Little Creek cleared his throat nervously. "Because he has the kind of magic that can kill."

"You're not serious?" Ryan asked.

"Oh yes, I am very serious. Not only does he have the kind of magic that can kill . . . but he does not hesitate to use it."

4

Swift Arrow
walked quickly through the heat of the day.
He prayed quietly, thinking and meditating
as he crossed the canyon floor. He passed a
dried-up riverbed and saw the skeleton of a
long-dead coyote. He wondered if the animal had died of thirst. Perhaps it had
crawled for miles to reach the river, only to
discover that it was bone-dry.

Swift Arrow stopped and looked down at the skeleton. His body grew tense. Carefully, he stooped down onto one knee for a closer look. There was something about the pattern of the bones on the sand. . . . It was the same jagged pattern that he had seen in the lightning.

Suddenly he was filled with anxiety. He couldn't explain it, but he was seized with the need to return to his village. To return at once. Swift Arrow turned and started for home.

As they moved along the ridge, Little Creek entertained Scott and Ryan by telling them various legends and stories. One of his favorites was the legend of Buffalo Cry. Buffalo Cry was a very strong brave who lived over a hundred summers ago. He was sent to bring the peace pipe to his enemies, but on the way a rattlesnake bit him. As he lay dying, he chanted to the eagle god. After he died, his spirit entered an eagle, which came and took the peace pipe from his hand and flew with it to the enemy tribe. When the rival chief saw the eagle carrying the Apache peace pipe, he declared peace between the two tribes. The peace lasted many years.

"So you really think Buffalo Cry's spirit entered the eagle?" Scott asked.

Little Creek shrugged. "The eagle did exactly as Buffalo Cry wished. Man cannot order a wild eagle."

"I suppose not," Scott agreed. "But maybe God just used the eagle to answer Buffalo Cry's prayer for peace."

"What's the difference?" Little Creek asked. "Whether God commanded the eagle or the spirit of the brave entered the eagle, it's all the same. Buffalo Cry's eagle brought peace between the tribes."

"I don't know," Scott said, shaking his head. "I just can't buy the idea of a person's spirit entering some animal. The Bible says when we die we go to face God, not hang out inside some eagle."

"I think it's kinda cool," Ryan said. "Just because it's different from the way we grew up doesn't mean it's wrong."

Before Scott could disagree, Little Creek continued, "It's the heart of shamanism. Shamans believe that by chanting and using certain herbs they can become one with the souls of animals, particularly the eagle, the wolf, and the lizard."

Again Scott shook his head. "Sorry, it's too weird for me."

Ryan didn't respond, but to Scott his silence said tons.

A moment later Ryan shouted, "Hey, check it out!" Scott and Little Creek turned, but Ryan was already scampering down the hill.

Scott looked to the bottom and saw a bunch of stones carefully laid out in some sort of pattern. It was almost as if they were spelling out words or forming crude stick figures. Intrigued, Scott also started down the hill.

"Wait," Little Creek called to them as he followed after Scott. "Be careful not to upset the stones. This is one of Dark Bear's holy places."

But Scott had already reached the bottom and begun hopping on the stones, jumping from one to the other. "I'm not hurting them," he said. "I won't mess them up."

"Scott," Ryan said, "you should really show more respect. I mean, what if somebody saw you?"

"Oh, all right," Scott sighed. "If it's that big of a deal, I'll get off."

He'd barely hopped off when they heard a loud cracking sound toward the top of the mountain. All three spun around to see a huge cloud of dust and debris billowing down the slope—directly toward them.

"It's an avalanche!" Little Creek cried. "Run!"

No one had to be told twice, but it was too close and coming too fast. In a matter of seconds the first of the boulders descended upon them.

Ryan was the first to be hit. A boulder the size of a basketball grazed his thigh. He let out a cry but continued running.

Scott was luckier. He dodged an even bigger rock that crashed into the ground immediately beside him. Soon rock and sand and dust surrounded the three. Through the thick, hazy cloud, Scott saw another boulder, several times larger than any other that had fallen. He leaped out of the way just as the two-ton rock bounced past, missing him by inches.

It ended almost as quickly as it had begun. Except for their coughing and gasping for breath, everything grew quiet.

"Everyone all right?" Little Creek called.

"Yeah," Scott answered, choking.

"We're OK," Ryan coughed.

The guys climbed out of the gravel and rocks, then looked back at where they had been standing. It was covered in rock. Coincidence? Maybe.

After a few moments, Ryan coughed and

said, "Well, I guess we should probably be heading back."

"Yes." Little Creek's agreement was quick. "I'm afraid we've offended the spirits. It would not be safe to continue."

" 'Offended the spirits,' " Scott scoffed. "You don't really believe that."

But Little Creek said nothing. Nor did Ryan. Instead, they turned and started climbing back up to the path. As they walked, Ryan turned around several times and looked back down at the pile of rocks. Scott couldn't be certain, but Ryan seemed strangely drawn to the place. Over the months the two of them had become good friends. And, like most good friends, each could often tell what the other was thinking. It was becoming more and more obvious to Scott that Ryan was getting caught up in the Indian myths and legends. And, while Scott knew this wasn't wrong, something about Ryan's fascination caused him concern.

"Hey—" Ryan stopped abruptly and pointed toward the top of the hill—"look."

Scott stopped and turned but saw nothing. "What?" he asked.

"He's gone now."

"There was somebody out here?"

Ryan nodded.

"Who?"

"I don't know . . . but he had something coming out of his head."

"Horns?" Little Creek asked. "Did they look like horns?"

"Well, yeah."

"Then we'd better hurry." Little Creek suddenly broke into a trot.

"Why?" Ryan asked, jogging beside him. "What's going on?"

"If what you saw were horns, then we'd better get out of here. Fast."

"But *why?*"

Little Creek didn't answer. "Come on," he insisted, continuing to run. "Come *on.*"

Scott didn't press the issue, and neither did Ryan. Whatever it was that Ryan had seen had made Little Creek pretty nervous. And whatever it was, neither Scott nor Ryan felt inclined to stick around and find out why.

An hour later as they approached camp, Little Creek said a hasty good-bye. He still would not tell them the reason for his concern, but it was obvious he was anxious to get away from them. Scott and Ryan wished him farewell and headed toward their tent.

As they walked up, a tantalizing aroma filled the air. "What's that smell?" Scott called. "I'm starved."

"You're *always* starved," Becka said as she

stooped over the grill to check on the thick, sizzling hamburgers.

"You boys are just in time for lunch," Mom called.

"Great," Ryan said.

"But look at you—you're filthy. What happened?"

"Oh, we just had a little run-in with a falling mountain," Scott quipped.

"You what?"

"We just had a little—"

"Never mind," Mom interrupted. "Go wash up. When you get back you can tell us all about it."

~

Becka watched the burgers carefully, making sure they didn't burn. When Scott and Ryan returned from washing up, she grinned. "It's about time! These things are ready to serve up."

"What do you boys want on them?" Mom asked.

"Oh . . . anything's fine," Ryan said.

"Yeah," Scott agreed. "Whatever you got."

"Whatever we've got?" Rebecca repeated, laughing. "That sounds pretty suspicious coming from someone who complains about everything."

"Who? Me?" Scott asked, pretending to sound indignant.

"Yeah, you."

The guys each grabbed a plate, bun, burger, and some chips before settling down at the picnic table near their tent.

"Still no sign of Swift Arrow," Rebecca sighed. "We checked, and he hasn't come back yet. Nothing to do but just keep waiting, I guess."

"That's OK with me," Scott said. "I've had enough excitement for one day."

"It's OK with me, too," Ryan agreed. "I'd say the longer we can stay here, the better."

Becka glanced at Ryan. The guy was practically beaming. As the sun reflected off his jet black hair, she couldn't help thinking how gorgeous he looked . . . and how lucky she was. For the past year their friendship had been growing stronger. Oh, sure, they'd had their disagreements, but something was growing between them. Something deep. Something so powerful that when Ryan looked at her a certain way, Becka felt herself become weak and trembly inside.

Now she crossed over and sat beside him as she had so many times before. But instead of turning to smile at her, he barely seemed to notice her.

"I'm really starting to enjoy this trip, too,"

she said. "It's different from the others. So quiet, so peaceful . . ."

Ryan nodded, but when she glanced into his eyes, hoping for that special connection they always shared, she saw that he wasn't even looking at her. Once again he was off somewhere. And once again she felt a twinge of jealousy. Was it her imagination, or was he purposely ignoring her? She tried to push the thought from her mind, but it kept returning. Finally she asked softly, "Ryan, is everything OK?"

As if coming back from a dream, Ryan turned to her and smiled. "OK?" he asked. "Sure, everything's fine. You're right—this place is incredible. There's nothing the matter at all."

"Unless you count the avalanche that almost killed us," Scott said with a chuckle. "Other than that, Ryan's right, nothing's the matter."

Becka looked at him, startled.

"Avalanche?" Mom asked. She seemed equally startled—and concerned.

Scotty nodded. And then, obviously enjoying his role as storyteller, he began to explain all that had happened to them . . . from Little Creek's warnings about Dark Bear to Scotty's playing on the holy stones to the avalanche and finally to the horned figure Ryan claimed to have seen on the top of the ridge.

"You saw a guy . . . with horns?" Becka asked, feeling a sense of cold dread fill her.

"Yeah." Ryan nodded. "I mean, it was pretty fast. One second he was there; the next he was gone. But I'm sure he had horns."

"I'm not sure what all this means," Mom said slowly, "but I think you kids had better be a lot more careful in the future."

The guys nodded, but Becka didn't respond. Ryan's last phrase had sent a chill shooting up her back and through her shoulders. It was part of her built-in warning system. One that she'd grown to trust through their many encounters with evil. She shifted her weight, trying to shake the feeling off, but it would not go away.

"What's wrong?" Ryan asked. "Are you all right?"

Becka swallowed hard and looked out at the rocks. "Yesterday . . . when I almost fell off that rope bridge . . ."

"Yeah?"

"When it was all over, I looked up. And, well, I thought it was my imagination, but now . . ." She looked down. "When I looked up, I saw somebody standing on the ridge above us."

"Really?"

Becka nodded. She tried to swallow again, but this time her mouth was bone-dry. "It was like you said, he was there only for a second and then he was gone."

As if sensing there was more, Ryan asked, "And . . . ?"

"And—" Rebecca finally raised her eyes to meet Ryan's—"on top of his head were two large horns."

5

It was early in the morning when Ryan awoke—around four o'clock, according to his watch. He listened carefully, sure he'd heard something. Of course, camping out in the New Mexico mountains meant you were bound to hear lots of strange noises during the night—the howl of a coyote, the hoot of an owl, the rhythmic buzz of countless, unknown insects. But this was slightly different.

Karahhh . . . Karahhh . . .

There it was again. Very nearby. Almost animal, but strangely human.

Karahhh . . . Karahhh . . .

Now Ryan was wide-awake. He thought of waking Scott but decided not to. After all, the sound wasn't particularly threatening— and he didn't want to seem foolish or afraid.

Karahhh . . . Karahhh . . .

Quietly Ryan unzipped his sleeping bag and crawled out. He slipped on his jeans and grabbed a long-sleeved shirt for a jacket. Ever so silently, he unzipped the tent flaps and stepped out into the shadows.

The air was cool and slightly sticky. And the smells. Sage and dust and a hundred others he couldn't recognize. The moon was nearly full, filling the desert and mountains with its light. Everything was so peaceful, so silent, so—

Karahhh . . . Karahhh . . .

Ryan felt his heart beat a little harder. It was definitely no animal he'd ever heard. And although he couldn't explain why, he felt that it was calling.

Calling to him.

He crossed the dozen or so yards to the entrance of the campground.

Karahhh . . . Karahhh . . .

It sounded like it came from the side of the road. Slowing to a stop, he paused to peer into the moonlight.

Nothing. It sounded so close, and yet there was nothing.

He took in a breath to steady himself, then kept going. Maybe it was a raccoon. Or maybe it was some kind of weird bird.

Karahhh . . . Karahhh . . .

No, that was no bird. And he was nearly on top of it.

He had reached the side of the road when he saw it. Something in the shadows. Something big. And it was moving!

"I knew you'd come."

Ryan let out a gasp as Little Creek stepped into the moonlight.

"You scared me half to death!" Ryan exclaimed.

Little Creek smiled, his white teeth gleaming in the light. "I summoned you the Indian way, and you came. You have the heart of an initiate."

"A what?"

"A potential brave. I have seen that you are someone who may truly understand and appreciate the ways of my people. I want to show you someplace special. Will you come with me?"

Something told Ryan to refuse. It was like someone tugging at his mind—a kind of warning. But Little Creek seemed so excited. . . . Before he knew it, Ryan was nodding. "Yeah. Sure."

Again Little Creek smiled. Without another word, he turned and started down the path. Ryan joined him.

An hour later they were walking past Dark Bear's holy place, the location of the avalanche. Ryan felt a slight chill as he looked down at the pile of rock and stone. Instinctively, he glanced up to the peak where he had seen the man with the horns, but no one was there. Maybe no one ever had been.

"This way," Little Creek called as he disappeared into some tall weeds.

Ryan turned off the road and followed.

"Be careful—the ground drops off here."

Ryan was grateful for the warning as the ground began such a sudden slope that he had to struggle to keep his balance.

At last, Little Creek called out, "Over here."

Ryan looked up to see the boy standing at the entrance to a small cave.

"It looks small now," Little Creek said, "but after a few feet inside you can stand up."

Once again Ryan felt that small tug, that sense of caution, of warning. And once again, he brushed it aside. What was wrong with checking out a cave?

"Come on." Little Creek motioned for Ryan to follow him inside. Ryan obeyed. He had to stoop to enter. Immediately, he felt a coolness—it was a good fifteen to twenty degrees cooler inside. What's more, it was pitch-black. Fortunately Little Creek had a small flashlight, and its light reflected off the walls and ceiling. The walls rose rapidly, and after half a dozen steps Ryan was able to stand.

"How far does this thing go?" he asked.

"A very long way," Little Creek replied. "This, too, is a holy place, so I must ask you not to show it to anyone. I'm showing it to you because I believe you have the mind to understand."

Ryan felt himself swell a little with pride. This was quite an honor Little Creek was bestowing on him. What other secrets did he have to share?

After several more feet, Little Creek finally came to a stop. "Over there," he said, motioning with his flashlight. "Look at that wall."

Ryan caught his breath. On the near wall was a crude painting of an Indian brandishing a long spear and stalking a buffalo. The painting could have been a thousand years old.

"This was painted by my ancestors," Little Creek said in almost a whisper. "We don't know when, but legend says the brave in the painting is Dark Bear's great-great-grand-father."

Ryan whistled softly. "It looks even older than that," he said quietly.

Little Creek chuckled. "Not if you believe the other legend."

"Other legend?"

"That, like Dark Bear, his grandfathers before him each lived to be a thousand years old."

Ryan looked at Little Creek. "They . . . what?"

Little Creek shrugged. "It's not impossible. Doesn't the Bible talk about people living that long?"

"Well . . . yes, but—"

"So if it's in the Bible, it's possible, isn't it?"

Ryan nodded slowly. He wasn't sure he believed Little Creek, but he didn't want to argue. After all, he was in a cave in the middle of the New Mexico desert, looking at a painting that was made thousands of years ago, listening to its legends—things just didn't get any cooler than this!

If only that small voice inside would stop

nudging him, making him feel guilty, saying he should be careful. . . .

He shook his head. It was a stupid feeling. There was nothing dangerous here. He was doing nothing wrong.

"Come with me," Little Creek said, breaking into Ryan's thoughts.

Ryan followed the boy as he turned and a few steps later rounded a small bend. The cave grew larger and larger. Now it was several times Ryan's height, and the ceiling grew higher with every step. Soon they'd entered a huge, magnificent cavern.

"This painting has even more color," Little Creek said as he flashed the light across the cavern to the far wall.

It was the portrait of a medicine man calling down lightning. All around him other Indians cowered in fear as the thunderbolt struck the ground.

"Is this a battle scene?" Ryan asked.

"No," Little Creek replied. "We call it The Wrath of Shaman. It's supposed to be an angry medicine man calling down fire on members of the tribe who disobeyed his council."

"Could he really do that?"

"It depends on the power of the shaman. Sometimes he also fasts and takes herbs to help him see."

"What do you mean, 'see'?"

"To see into the netherworld, the spirit world."

Ryan felt a sudden chill. But this time it had nothing to do with the temperature inside the cave.

Little Creek continued, "Sometimes the shaman can see the cause of a sickness or the path to solve another person's problem."

"The herbs can help him do that?" Ryan asked.

Little Creek nodded. "The herbs clear his mind of the things of this world so he can focus on the supernatural. They help him get in touch with the Great Spirit."

Ryan said nothing as they made their way out of the cave, but during the trip back to the camp, he asked Little Creek if he would teach him more about the ways of his tribe.

"Sure." Little Creek grinned. "It's like I said—I think you have the potential of a brave."

Once again Ryan felt the pride swelling inside his chest.

Little Creek continued, "You should try some of the tea we drink at ceremony. I bet you could also see into the supernatural."

There was that nervous feeling again, but this time it was easy to shove it aside. There were far too many questions, too many new things to explore, to let his nerves stop him now. "Can't you see into the supernatural without the tea?"

"Some can," Little Creek answered. "But Dark Bear is the only one I know who can communicate with the Great Spirit without it."

Ryan nodded. After a while he turned to his little friend with a question—a question that had been forming in his mind most of the morning. "Little Creek?"

"Yes?"

"Do you think this Great Spirit you're always talking about . . . do you think that's just another name for God?"

Little Creek smiled. "Sure. What else could it be?"

As the boys returned to the camp, the sun was just cresting over the eastern ridge. It was a beautiful, golden dawn. And there, in the distance, a dark speck was walking toward them.

"Is that . . . ?" Ryan asked. "Is that Dark Bear?"

Little Creek slowed and peered into the distance. "No," he said, shaking his head. "It's Swift Arrow. He has finally returned from his time of seeking."

"Great," Ryan exclaimed, "that's the guy

we're supposed to talk to. Now we'll finally find out why we were sent here."

"I'm sure he's been fasting," Little Creek said. "Why don't you invite him to join your group for breakfast?"

"Good idea."

~

An hour later Mom was dishing up bacon and eggs for the group and their newest acquaintance, Swift Arrow.

As they sat around the picnic table eating, Becka couldn't help noticing how lean and muscular Swift Arrow was. As far as she could tell, the brave didn't have an ounce of fat on him.

"So," Scott asked as Becka passed around seconds, "are you a friend of Z's?"

Swift Arrow frowned. "I'm sorry. I don't recognize the name."

"Z," Scott repeated.

Swift Arrow shook his head.

"Do you surf much?"

Again Swift Arrow looked confused. "There are no large bodies of water near here. . . . Even the river is dried up, so it would be diffi-cult to—"

"No, no," Ryan chuckled. "He doesn't mean surf, like ride a board. He means, do you surf the Net? You know, visit the Internet with your computer?"

Swift Arrow grinned at the mistake. "I'm afraid I don't have a computer. Why do you ask?"

"That's where we met Z," Scott explained. "On the Net."

"At least that's where we think we met him," Becka corrected. "But he seems to know so much personal stuff about us that we suspect we might have run into him before."

"He's never told you who he is?"

"That's right." Becka nodded. "Which is one of the things that makes him so mysterious."

"That and the fact that he sends us all around the world to help folks out," Scott added.

"Well, I don't know why this Z has sent you," Swift Arrow said. "But I'm glad you came. For the past three days, I have been walking and praying, seeking for just such guidance. You are the answer to my prayers."

"How can these help?" Rebecca asked, pleased but confused by the young man's obvious relief.

"Two years ago I left the reservation and went to the university. During that time I became a Christian—"

"No kidding?" Scott interrupted. "We're all Christians, too."

"That's great." Swift Arrow grinned.

"Go on," Becka said. "You were walking and praying because . . ."

Swift Arrow nodded. "When I returned to my village after college, I was very anxious to share the things I'd learned about Jesus. Like many Native Americans, I had grown up thinking that Jesus was a white man's God, opposed to everything we believed. But that's not true. Many of Christ's teachings fit in with what I have learned from nature, from *his* creation. In fact, the gospel actually completes our teachings . . . helping us make sense out of them. It also helped me understand what parts of the old teachings were true and what parts were not."

"I'll bet you found a lot that was true," Ryan said.

Becka glanced at him. She knew Ryan had developed a real interest in and appreciation for these people, and that was good. But it seemed he was going beyond that—as though he was trying to rationalize that all Native American beliefs were the same as Christianity.

"Yes, some things are the same," Swift Arrow answered. Then he hesitated, as though unsure if he should go on.

"Please," Mom urged him quietly, "tell us what happened."

He nodded and continued, "When I arrived home, I was not able to share these new truths with my people. They were so worried about the drought. It consumed their every thought. I tried praying with some of them, but the rain did not come, and soon they lost interest in my prayers. And my faith."

"I'm sorry to hear that," Becka said.

"But there's more. Last week the tribal shaman, Dark Bear, began saying that my return to the village had actually prolonged the drought. That I had brought a plague onto the village because of my belief in the white man's religion."

"That's terrible," Scott protested.

Rebecca glanced at Scott, nodding in agreement. That's when she saw it—another storm cloud starting to form off in the distance, toward the southwest. It was similar to the huge thunderhead that had brought the wind the day they'd come to the village—the wind that had nearly knocked her off the bridge. She felt a little knot of uneasiness grow inside.

"The drought has greatly tested my faith," Swift Arrow continued. "I went on the walkabout to fast and pray for God to show me what to do. I want to share my faith with the people, but it is hard for minds to be open when bellies are empty."

Becka glanced back at the cloud. It continued its slow approach.

"We are running out of the grain we've stored, and there are no new crops. Unless it rains, we will have to abandon this, the home of our forefathers."

"That would be awful," Ryan protested.

Swift Arrow nodded. "It is either that or starve."

"There must be something you can do," Mom said.

"Dark Bear claims I have rejected the faith of my people. I want to challenge him, to prove that he is wrong and that God has far greater power than he does. But until now I have been afraid."

"Until now?" Becka asked.

Swift Arrow nodded and smiled. "Now four strangers come—strangers who share my faith. It is the sign I was hoping for."

"I still don't understand," Rebecca said. "What exactly do you think we can do about a drought?"

"Hold that thought," Mom said as she crossed to the fire to scoop up more eggs. She passed around the food and everyone, including Becka, dug in. It was surprising how the fresh air and exercise increased their appetites.

"This is very good," Swift Arrow said.

"Yeah, Mom," Scott agreed. "Good job."

Rebecca nodded and noticed that the thunderhead was much closer. She was surprised at how quickly clouds formed and moved through these parts.

"Go ahead," Ryan urged Swift Arrow. "You were telling us about the drought."

"To me yoiur arrival is a sign that I must take a stand against Dark Bear. I must tell the truth about the Christian God, and then the drought will end. Because once I have—"

But Swift Arrow never finished. Suddenly there was an explosion, a thunderclap so loud that it shook the table. All five of them jumped and looked up at the sky.

Scott was the first to spot him. It was the same man she had seen from the bridge. The same one Ryan had said he'd seen at the avalanche. He stood high above them, on the very top of Starved Rock. He was wearing a buffalo headdress, complete with horns. And even from that distance it was possible to see his piercing stare, glaring down at them.

"Dark Bear," Swift Arrow whispered.

Several seconds passed, with only the echoing roll of thunder in the background. And then, ever so slowly, Dark Bear began to chant, and to dance in a small circle atop the rock.

Rebecca turned to Swift Arrow. She wanted to ask what Dark Bear was doing, but the expression on the young man's face stopped her cold. Fear. No, worse than fear . . . terror.

Swift Arrow glanced back up at the sky; then he leaped up from the table and shouted, "Get away from the table! Everybody get away!"

The panic in his voice spurred the others to move.

"Jump back!" he shouted. "Get away from the table! Do it now!"

"Hurry!" Swift Arrow shouted, grabbing Mom and Becka by the arms, pulling them away. *"Get back! Get back!"*

Ryan and Scott followed suit, although not without the usual questions: "What's going on? What's wrong?"

Before Swift Arrow could answer, the sky was filled with a tremendous, blinding flash. Becka and Mom screamed. Air crackled and burned all around them. Suddenly there was a powerful blast—an explosion of thunder so intense that it knocked all five of them to the ground.

And then it was over, as quickly as it had

begun. Only the echo of thunder against the hills—and the ringing in their ears—remained.

"What . . . what happened?" Scott stammered as he struggled to his feet.

"I think we were almost hit by lightning!" Mom answered, her voice shaking.

"Look at that!" Ryan exclaimed. He was pointing to the table and benches. Or to what was left of them. The table was split in two. The benches were cracked and tipped over, and all of the wood was charred.

Not only were they charred, but they were smoldering, too.

A shaken Becka looked over at Swift Arrow, who was rising to his feet. He was trembling. He did not say a word. He only tilted his head and looked back up at the top of Starved Rock.

Becka followed his gaze. There was Dark Bear, standing with his arms folded across his chest, glowering down at them. Her eyes darted back to Swift Arrow. "Did he do that?" she asked incredulously. "He couldn't have done that, could he?"

Swift Arrow tried to answer, but no words came. Becka watched him swallow and try again. Still nothing. All he could do was stare.

And then Becka heard another voice—distant, but heavy and full of ominous authority.

"Let this be a warning!" It was Dark Bear, calling down from the rock. "A warning to you all. It is *I* who commune with the gods of nature. It is *I* who will make the rain. And all who oppose me or my magic . . . will surely die."

6

It was huge. In fact, it seemed to Becka that it was as tall as the mountains themselves, though she knew that was impossible. Still, the eagle's wings covered most of the sky as it cast its shadow on the desert floor. Rebecca stared, trying to grasp its size, when the giant bird spotted them.

Instantly, it began to dive. Already Becka suspected she was dreaming . . . but it seemed so real. And the bird was so big. She tried to wake herself, but it was no use. The bird continued its dive.

"Run!" she shouted to Ryan. *"Run!"*

"But it's only a dream," Ryan protested.

"It doesn't matter. Run!"

She started off, but Ryan refused to move. Reluctantly, she doubled back and grabbed his arm. She tugged, but he wouldn't move. The eagle was still some way off, but it was coming in fast. And it was screaming. Under its cry she could hear the wind whizzing past the giant wings as they cut through the air.

Rebecca tugged again until Ryan finally started to move. Now they were holding hands, racing across the desert floor, heading for a clump of trees. She glanced over her shoulder. The bird was gaining on them. She knew they would never make it. Even if they did, she doubted the trees would offer much protection against such a creature.

All at once her legs grew heavy. Dead weight. But she had to keep going, even if it was only a dream. She knew that if she slowed down the bird would attack and rip them to pieces.

Then everything went black. She and Ryan were still running—she could feel her legs moving, hear Ryan gasping beside her—but they were running in darkness!

Again she tried to force herself awake, and again she failed.

They continued running. Her lungs burned for air; her cheeks were streaked with tears of hopelessness. And then she saw it. Sensed it, really. The great claw of the beast dropping down, reaching out for Ryan.

"Don't worry," he shouted, "it's only a dream!"

The talons reached out and closed around his neck. Rebecca screamed and watched in horror as the talons tore into him, lifting him high into the air.

She screamed again, but it did no good. Then, suddenly, the eagle disappeared, and Rebecca was all alone. In the dark. Gasping for breath . . .

She heard the sound of insects buzzing outside her tent and, off in the distance, the lone call of an eagle.

She was awake. Or was she? Becka lay there, unsure. She looked around her tent. The dream was over. At least, she thought it had been a dream. But if she'd been dreaming, then what about the eagle call she'd just heard?

With more than a little anxiety, Rebecca climbed out of her sleeping bag and pulled on her jeans. She unzipped the tent. It was still dark outside, but as far as she could tell, there were no giant eagles hovering in the sky. She stepped outside and crept over to Scotty and Ryan's tent. Already she could hear Scotty snoring away. It was a sound she was all too familiar with, but one that, at least for now, she found very comforting.

Carefully she peeked into their tent. There was Scotty, all right, sprawled out and snoring to beat the band. But where was Ryan? There was no sign of him. Only a ripped sleeping bag and his torn and shredded clothing . . . and feathers, lots and lots of giant eagle feathers.

Becka covered her mouth to stifle a scream. And then she saw it, high overhead: a giant eagle swooping down out of the darkness. It was coming at her. She tried to run but was paralyzed. She opened her mouth to scream, but no sound would come. And then . . .

She forced herself awake.

This time it was real. But just to be sure, she reached out to pinch her arm. Hard. The shock of pain was a comforting confirmation. Yes, she was awake. She was in her tent, inside her sleeping bag, trying to catch her breath.

"Beck?" She heard a whisper. "Becka, are

you all right?" It was Ryan. He was just out-side her tent. A wave of relief washed over her.

"Becka?"

"Yeah," she whispered. "Hang on, I'll be right there."

Quickly she slipped out of her sleeping bag and into her jeans and shirt, threw open the tent, and raced into his arms. "Oh, Ryan!" She was practically sobbing.

"Are you all right?" he asked again with surprise.

"I thought you were eaten . . . or got snatched up by the eagle or . . . or . . ." She knew she wasn't making much sense, but it didn't matter. The important thing was that Ryan was all right.

"What eagle?" he asked. "What are you talking about?"

"Nothing," she said, taking a deep breath and forcing the last of the sleep from her mind. "It was a dream . . . a dream inside of a dream. And I knew it was a dream, but still—everything seemed so real." Once again she hugged him, grateful to feel his arms around her.

"It's all right, Beck," he said, almost chuck-ling. "I'm OK. Really."

At last she pulled back to look at him, to

gaze into those deep blue eyes. "What are you doing outside at this time of night?"

He shrugged. "I was just enjoying the view . . . until I heard you calling. Look—" he motioned toward the sky—"take a look at those stars, will you? Have you ever seen anything more beautiful?"

Rebecca tilted her head back to look up into the night. The sky glowed with stars. They looked so close it was as if the surrounding peaks nearly touched them.

"I thought I'd take a walk up to the ridge again. You want to come along?" he asked.

"Sure. I'm so wound up about that dream, I don't think I'd be able to get back to sleep anyway."

Ryan looked at her and smiled. It was the smile that always melted her. The one that made her legs just a little bit weak. She could never figure out if he knew when he was using it or not. She coughed slightly and tried to change the subject.

"Is Scotty still asleep?"

"Yeah, he was up most of the night, down at the general store, trying to get ahold of Z."

Rebecca looked at him, a quick hope stirring inside her. "Did he?"

Ryan shook his head. "He got the modem all set up, but Z never came on-line."

"Oh," Rebecca said, disappointed.

"But there was a message waiting."

"What did it say?"

"Not much. Just a Bible verse and a note to call back tomorrow."

"A Bible verse?"

"Uh-huh."

"Which one?"

"Here, I wrote it down."

Becka waited as he reached into his shirt pocket and unfolded a piece of paper.

"It's from Timothy. Here . . . 'In the last times some will turn away from what we believe; they will follow lying spirits and teachings that come from demons.'"

They both stared at the paper for a moment.

"Have any idea what it means?" Ryan looked at her curiously.

Rebecca frowned. "No. Do you?"

He shook his head, and they stared at the verse again. Finally Ryan sighed and folded it back up. "Well, Z will probably fill us in on it tomorrow."

Becka nodded. "I hope so."

Becka laced her arm through Ryan's, and they started their walk toward the ridge. The gorgeous New Mexico mountains, the full moon, an incredible-looking and super-caring boyfriend on her arm . . . these were the types of moments she dreamed of. Unfortunately there was another dream still clinging to the back of her mind. This had been the second dream of an eagle attack. What did it mean? And what did that Bible verse mean?

As if that weren't enough to worry about, there was Ryan. He was different. Ever since they'd arrived here, he seemed to be growing more distant. The fact that he rarely looked at her was one thing. The fact that they'd barely had a conversation in two days was another. It was as though everything about this place—the mountains, the village, the people, their beliefs—fascinated him so much that he barely acknowledged she was there.

All right, maybe she was just being overly sensitive. It wouldn't be the first time. Or worse yet, maybe she was jealous—but . . . of what?

They walked together in silence for several minutes as she debated whether or not to talk to him about her worries—but she had never been one to keep her feelings too tightly wrapped. "Ryan, are you all right?"

He nodded slightly but did not look at her.

"Ryan?"

"Hmm? Oh—yeah?" He gave her a sheepish smile. "Sorry, Beck. What did you say?"

She softly repeated the question. "Is everything OK?"

He nodded. "It's just this place. . . . I mean it's so . . . mysterious and wonderful. It can get a guy thinking, that's all."

"About what?" she asked quietly. "Thinking about what?"

"Nothing." He shrugged. "Nothing, really . . . and everything."

These were not exactly the kinds of answers that made her quit worrying. What *was* he thinking about? Her? Them? Or was it something else? something even deeper? She'd noticed that he hadn't cracked open his Bible once since they'd arrived. Back in the beginning, when he'd first become a Christian, he practically devoured the thing. Back then, he was full of so many questions and he was always studying the Bible to find answers. But now . . .

She wanted to ask him about a whole lot more—including their relationship—but Becka knew better than to throw herself at Ryan. It was important to give him his space, to let him work things out.

Still . . .

Her thoughts were interrupted by a shooting star that blazed through the eastern sky. It looked as if a Fourth of July sparkler were trying to light the entire sky before it burned out. Too soon, it faded from sight.

"There's something . . ." Ryan cleared his

throat and started again. "There's something about this place, these people . . ."

Rebecca listened intently.

"The way they live off the land—no cars, no factories. It's so honest that it makes our money-grubbing way of life look pretty sick by comparison. I mean, they're such a noble people."

Rebecca nodded. She had to give him that. She also wanted to mention that these very same people were starving because they'd based their entire economy on rainfall in the desert, but when someone is waxing emotional, logic is usually an unwelcome guest.

"And when I hear Little Creek talk about the Great Spirit and nature and Mother Earth . . . I'm not so sure they're all that wrong. I mean, there's certainly nothing evil about respecting the earth and treating her correctly."

Rebecca nodded again. "Respecting the earth is a very good thing. It's worshiping it that gets to be the problem."

Ryan looked at her strangely, then smiled. "I think you're just afraid because this is all so new to you."

Becka started to answer, then thought better of it. She was afraid, all right, but not because things were new. After all, she and her brother had spent most of their lives in the South American rain forests, living around people who worshiped nature and believed in animal spirits. Shamanism was nothing new to her. The vocabulary and details might be a little different, but for Becka many of the things she'd been seeing and hearing were all too familiar.

She wasn't afraid for herself. She threw another look at Ryan. She wasn't afraid for herself at all.

~

Scott heard the commotion before he was really awake. Several of the people from the village were nearby, talking in loud voices. He rolled over to see that Ryan had already gone. He roused himself enough to hear what the people were saying. A few were speaking English, but most spoke a language he couldn't understand. He did, however, make out occasional English phrases like "big meeting," "time something was done," and "full moon."

Whatever they were discussing, it sounded important. So Scott quickly rose, got dressed, and stepped into the morning light.

The group was a few dozen feet away, walking past the campground toward the village. Little Creek was trailing along behind them.

"Hey, Scott! What's up?" he asked when he caught sight of Scott.

Scott shrugged. "You tell me."

"Dark Bear has called a council meeting on the first night of the full moon. That's two days from now. He wants to have Swift Arrow expelled from the village."

"What?" Scott said.

"And there's more. He wants to throw you guys out with him."

"You're kidding me."

Little Creek shook his head. "Nope, that's what it says."

Feeling his face start to burn with anger and unsure what to do, Scott turned back to his tent and pulled out his sleeping bag to start rolling it up. "I'd like to see him try," he snorted. "Just cause ole Antler Head can do special effects with lightning doesn't mean he has any power over us."

"You're in his village," Little Creek replied simply. "He has the power. Besides, I would think that after last night, you would have stopped mocking his power."

Scott paused and looked back up at Little Creek. "I'm not mocking his power. I'm just not quaking in fear over it." He turned back to his sleeping bag and continued rolling it up. "Besides, if you ask me—"

Suddenly he stopped midsentence. There,

inches from his hand, was a rattlesnake crawling out of the folds of his sleeping bag.

"Careful . . . Don't move," Little Creek whispered. "That one is deadly."

Scott froze, holding his breath as the snake's tongue darted in and out and the creature slithered even closer to his outstretched fingers. Any second it would strike. Any second it would—

Shuuuushing!

A steel-tipped arrow hit its mark, flying directly between Scott's fingers and straight into the snake's head. The darting tongue ceased its movement.

Scott stared in astonishment, his usually witty brain numb; his usually smart mouth dumb.

"Didn't get you, did it?" Swift Arrow asked.

Scott slowly turned to see Swift Arrow standing on a slight ridge, about twenty feet away. True to his name, the young man had fired the arrow and killed the snake just as it was about to strike.

"No . . . ," Scott half spoke, half wheezed. "I'm fine." He swallowed hard. "Just fine . . ."

"That was close," Little Creek said, marveling. "Nice shot."

Swift Arrow nodded a thank-you and approached. "I suppose you saw these notices," he said to Scott while pointing to the yellow sheet in Little Creek's hand.

Scott nodded, still not sure if he had a voice. But he gave it a try. "What . . . what are you going to do?"

Swift Arrow seemed to wilt slightly. "I'm not sure. Perhaps I heard the Lord wrong. Perhaps I am causing more trouble here than good."

Scott shook his head. "When things start going nuts around you, sometimes that means you're on the right track."

"But sometimes it can mean you are not in God's will."

Scott nodded. "Maybe. All I'm saying is don't be so quick to give up. Haven't you been doing what you know is right?"

Swift Arrow nodded. "Yes. I've followed what I believe is true, but . . ."

"But what?"

"But Dark Bear has very strong medicine."

"It may be strong, but it's not right."

Swift Arrow shook his head. "I don't know. I mean . . . much of the way he believes is how I grew up."

Scott carefully searched the young man's face before he continued. "Do you believe the spirit of a human can go into an eagle? Do you believe that the earth is something to worship?"

Swift Arrow shook his head. "No. But I know that my grandfather, like most of the tribe, based his life on such beliefs. And my father, he believes some of the legends still. Besides, it's not just a question of what I believe. Little by little my people are adopting the white man's ways. We are a disappearing people."

"Things aren't like that," Scott argued. "If something is true, then it's true, and if it's not, then it's not. It doesn't matter whose grandfather believed what."

Swift Arrow shook his head. "Only a white man would say something like that."

"But you can't believe something just because your grandfather believed it. That doesn't make sense. Don't let that trick you into running away."

Swift Arrow nodded slowly. "Much of what you say is true. Maybe . . . maybe I'm just afraid."

"Well now, being afraid is something I can relate to." Scott grinned. He couldn't help throwing a look over to the charred remains of the picnic table. "And there's nothing wrong with being afraid, especially when it comes to this kind of stuff. But God can handle even our fear. If we let him."

Swift Arrow stared at Scott for a long moment. Finally he spoke. "I don't know

how you people came to me. I don't know
who this Z is—though I have a friend into
computers with whom I have spoken about
these problems. Perhaps he knows your Z.
Then again, maybe you are simply angels
who have come to help me."

"Whoa!" Scott protested. "I'm no angel."

"That's for sure!"

Scott turned to see Becka and Ryan
approaching from the road.

Swift Arrow laughed. "Maybe not, but you
bring messages from on high, and they help
keep me to the path."

"We call that being a friend," Scott said
with a grin.

Swift Arrow returned the smile, but it
slowly faded, and he let out a long sigh.
"Well then, my friends, I must tell you. This
friend of yours is afraid. He is afraid to face
Dark Bear, and he is afraid not to."

Later that evening, Mom, Rebecca, and
Scott stood around the telephone, which
rested on the worn wooden counter of the
general store. Scott had his laptop up and
running, trying to contact Z.

"After all," he said, punching up the number, "Z's the one who got us into this mess.

Hopefully he'll have an idea how to get us out."

Rebecca nodded and glanced out the window. The sun had already set, and it was getting steadily darker. "I just wish Ryan were here," she said quietly. "This could be real important."

"He's out with Little Creek looking at more Indian stuff," Scott said as he typed away.

"Again?" Rebecca sighed.

"I know," Scott agreed. "It's like the guy can never get enough. He loves everything about Indians. What they eat, where they live, what they believe . . ."

"That's what I mean," Rebecca said. "It's like he's completely carried away with it. I just wish he were here to talk to Z."

"I do too. But if Swift Arrow's going to do anything before Dark Bear's council, it should be soon. We'll just have to fill Ryan in later."

Becka nodded. She knew Scotty was right. She just wished he weren't.

Moments later the familiar Internet logo came up on the laptop screen.

"Got him!" Scott exclaimed. "We're both on-line."

Mom and Becka moved in closer to watch. They'd talked to Z dozens of times and had received dozens of pieces of advice. But contacting the mysterious stranger was always an important event for them. One they never seemed to tire of.

After Scott filled Z in on all that had happened, there was a long pause. Finally the words of Z's answer began to form:

There is a spiritual battle raging. Much is at stake. Swift Arrow has been called to bring his people the gospel. Dark Bear will never allow it.

Scott reached for the keyboard and typed:

Then what should we do?

As they waited for a reply, there was a rumble of thunder in the distance. Becka glanced out the window. "Looks like the wind's picking up."

As if in answer, there was another flash of lightning, followed in a few seconds by a much louder clap of thunder.

Scott sighed impatiently. "What's taking him so long to respond?" For the briefest second the lights in the store dimmed and the computer screen flickered. "Oh no," Scott groaned.

"What's wrong?" Mom asked.

"The phone line may be going." But the

screen stabilized, and Scott said, "It's coming back." And then a moment later, "Ah, here we go."

Once again Becka leaned forward to read the words as they came on:

You have encountered situations similar to this. You know your authority. Swift Arrow need not be afraid. However, be careful not to underestimate Dark Bear's power.

Scott and Becka exchanged glances. But Z wasn't finished.

Did you receive the Bible verse?

Scott typed:

Yes, but we didn't understand. Who's it for? What does it mean?

Once again the lights and the screen flickered, and once again power returned. Mom, Becka, and Scott watched as Z's answer formed:

You are waging two battles. One is offense, the other defense. I am very concerned that one of you is about to fall. And if one falls, you all will fall.

Quickly Scott typed:

Who are you concerned about?

There was no answer. Scott tried again.

Z? Z, who are you concerned about?

And then once again the verse formed.

"In the last times some will turn away from what
we believe; they will follow lying spirits and
teachings that come from demons."
1 Timothy 4:1

Scott let out a sigh of frustration and
typed:

*Yes, yes, we have that verse, but what are we
supposed to—*

Scott never finished. There was another
flash of lightning, and the telephone line
went dead. The computer was disconnected.

7

The next morning Swift Arrow came to their camp at daybreak. "I have decided to call a council of my own a day before Dark Bear's. I will speak to the people about my beliefs."

"Hey, that's great," Scott said.

Swift Arrow nodded. "But I need your help to get the word out."

"We can do that," Rebecca said. "When will it be?"

"It must be tonight. For it is tomorrow that Dark Bear will try to incite the people to drive us out."

Scott and Becka agreed to spend the morning going through the village and telling everyone about the meeting. At least that was their plan. Unfortunately they ended up spending most of that time looking for Ryan. Apparently he'd taken off before sunrise with Little Creek, and no one knew where they had gone. And now Becka wasn't just kind of worried. She was really worried.

"This is a waste of time," Scott complained. "We need to tell the village about Swift Arrow's council. We'd better forget about Ryan until later."

Rebecca sighed. Forgetting about Ryan was the last thing she wanted to do, but she knew her little brother had a point. "I suppose you're right. I just feel like he should be with us, that's all."

Scott nodded. "I know. But we'll look for him later. I promise."

It didn't take long for the two to visit the people of the village. In less than an hour they had nearly finished going up and down the rows of small homes, speaking to the people they met. Whenever they encountered a villager who didn't speak English, they showed a message Swift Arrow had written out for them in the tribal language. In fact, they were showing this very note to an old woman when Dark Bear himself stepped out from behind the door of the house.

When Becka saw the shaman, she went cold. He looked even more menacing close-up than when he was perched high atop the rock. He approached them, his eyes steely and full of rage. Instinctively Scott and Rebecca stepped back.

"Depart from here," he growled. "This is not your battle. It's about the ways of my people."

It took Becka a moment to find her voice. When she did, she was surprised at how even and controlled it sounded. "No. That's not all that this is about."

"Beck . . . ," Scott warned.

But she had already started, and there was no backing down. "It's about truth. Spiritual truth. And that is the same for everyone."

Dark Bear glared at her. "You risk much, girl. . . . This is not your fight."

Rebecca was breathing harder now, but she forced herself to continue, trying to stay collected and calm. "Listen, Mr. . . . Dark Bear. Why don't you come to Swift Arrow's council tonight? Not to fight, but just to listen to what he says. Later, after you've heard Swift Arrow's side, maybe you can decide what's really right for your people to believe."

She waited for an answer as Dark Bear's eyes shifted from her to Scotty. She wasn't sure what he was looking at . . . until she heard the choking sounds.

She turned to see Scott holding his throat with both hands. He was gasping for breath.

"Scott!" she cried. "Scotty, what's wrong?"

But Scott couldn't answer. All he could do was gasp, pointing to his throat, trying to catch his breath.

Becka spun back to Dark Bear. She'd seen this before, in past encounters. And she knew the solution. The shaman's gaze was fierce, intimidating, but she knew who had the real authority. "Release him!" she ordered.

Dark Bear glared at her, but she would not back down. "In the name and power of the Lord Jesus Christ, I command you to release him."

At first Dark Bear smiled, but then, as Rebecca stood her ground, he realized she meant business. Slowly his smile faded.

Scott coughed loudly and started breathing, dragging in deep gulps of air. Becka glanced at him. She knew the choking was a tactic to try to scare them. But she also knew that, because they were committed believers in Christ, Dark Bear had no real power over them. These were just more "special effects" in an attempt to frighten them. And they weren't going to work.

Becka smiled at Scott, and he nodded. They turned to face Dark Bear, to continue the encounter . . . but the medicine man had disappeared.

Ryan and Little Creek sat cross-legged in the coolness of the cave. Little Creek had lit a small lantern, and the light hit the wall. Immediately, the painting of the great warrior hunting the buffalo appeared in the light. Ryan stared intently at the warrior's face. Was Dark Bear really a direct descendant of this brave as he'd claimed?

Ryan's thoughts were interrupted as Little Creek took a small flask from his shirt pocket. "It's the tea I told you about," he said, smiling.

"Tea?" Ryan repeated.

"Yes, remember? I said it will help you better hear the call of the Great Spirit." He leaned toward Ryan and held the flask out.

Ryan hesitated.

"Don't worry. There is only a small amount of the red berries in this mixture."

"Red berries?" Ryan asked, staring at the flask.

"Yes. It is berries that give the tea its hallucinogenic powers. I just put a little bit in because this is your first time. It won't hurt you, honest."

Again Little Creek held it out to him, and again Ryan hesitated.

"It's OK. I promise. You're a spiritual person, Ryan. It will be easy for you to contact the Great Spirit, but you must do so with the tea."

The little tug hit Ryan again, telling him it was wrong, to be careful. . . . But weren't they all talking about the same God, the one and only 'Great Spirit'? And if this were really a way to connect with God, if he could combine the best of both worlds—his Christian faith and this spiritual ritual with the tea—then what was the harm?

Little Creek continued holding the flask out to him. "If you really want to understand our ways, this is the fastest and easiest method. Please, it is OK. I promise."

Ryan watched as his hand reached out to take the flask. It was almost like watching someone else. Then he raised it to his lips. He hesitated and looked at Little Creek one last time. The boy smiled, and Ryan opened his mouth to drink the tea.

For a while nothing happened. As before, they discussed the history of Little Creek's tribe, his beliefs, and his heritage. Then Ryan felt a wave of dizziness. At first he shrugged it off. They had left camp before breakfast, and he was getting pretty hungry. It was only natural that he would feel a little light-headed.

Then he noticed something else. On the cave painting. He hadn't seen it before, but in the right-hand corner, perched on a cliff, was an eagle. It was so small, it was no wonder he hadn't noticed it before. But as he watched, the bird started to grow.

Ryan turned to Little Creek and tried to tell him, but the words wouldn't come. "Thhhhe painttttting . . ." was all he managed to slur.

Little Creek smiled. "Relax, my friend. The tea is taking effect. Focus inward, and see what the Great Spirit will show you."

Ryan couldn't focus on anything. He felt like he was going to throw up. His head began to spin, and his stomach started to churn. When he looked back at the painting, the eagle was as large as the hunter. What was worse, its wings were moving!

Ryan closed his eyes, hoping to force him-

self back into reality. It was as if he were looking over the edge of a very high cliff or stum-
bling through a dark tunnel knowing that
there was a great hole somewhere in front of
him . . . a huge chasm that went on forever.
If he wasn't careful, he would stumble and
fall to certain death.

When he reopened his eyes, the eagle was
so large that one of its wings pushed out of
the painting, extending across the cave wall.

Ryan's heart began to pound. He started
breathing rapidly. What if the drug didn't
wear off? What if it damaged him? What if
he had to live like this, with his brain scram-
bled, for the rest of his life?

Or, worse yet, what if the images he was
seeing were real?

All of these thoughts froze when the eagle
turned its lifeless eye directly toward him. It
had seen him. Ryan was sure of it. Just as he
was sure that it wanted him. Slowly, with
great effort, it detached itself from the wall
and started flying toward him.

With open beak, it drew closer and closer.
Ryan covered his face. And still, somehow,
he could see it coming—its jet black, lifeless
eyes growing larger and larger as it flew
closer. Suddenly Ryan realized it wasn't the
creature's beak but its eye that was going to

devour him. That eye was going to absorb him, swallow him. . . .

The eye . . . the eye . . . the eye . . . the eye . . .

᠕

Two hours later, Ryan woke up. He lay outside the cave, vaguely aware that Little Creek was wiping his forehead with a damp handkerchief.

"How are you feeling?" Little Creek asked.

Ryan bobbed his head. "I don't know. Woozy, I guess. How did I get out here?"

"You got up and started to run. We were just sitting there looking at the painting when you jumped up and tried to run. You managed a few steps before you crashed into the wall. It knocked you out cold."

Ryan winced as he touched the lump on his forehead. "That would explain this headache."

"I carried you out here hoping the fresh air and sunlight would help. You've been sleeping for a long time."

Ryan nodded. Already memories of the vision were returning. "I—I saw an eagle," he stammered.

"An eagle?" Little Creek's mouth dropped open. "Really?"

Ryan nodded. "It flew out of the painting right at me."

"There is no eagle in that painting," Little Creek said, unable to hold back his excitement.

"But I'm sure—"

"No, no, but this is a wondrous sign. The Great Spirit is sending the eagle to you. This means he has much to teach you!"

"Really?"

Little Creek nodded and smiled broadly. "I was right! You *are* an initiate. The Great Spirit will use you in many ways. Congratulations!" Little Creek extended his hand toward Ryan.

Ryan looked at it for a moment and then shook it warmly. "Thanks," he murmured. It was hard not to catch Little Creek's excitement. So he had been chosen. Chosen by the Great Spirit himself. And the eagle, the eagle was coming . . . coming just for him!

~

As evening approached, most of the village turned out for Swift Arrow's council. Scott and Rebecca stayed in the background since they didn't want their friendship with him to cause a problem. He had already been accused of following the ways of the white man, and having two white kids by his side probably wouldn't help him much. Still, from their vantage point they could see most of the tribe and enjoy looking at all the ceremonial clothing.

"I wish Ryan were here," Rebecca sighed for the hundredth time. "He would love this."

"Yeah," Scott said, barely listening. "Check out that fellow over there. He must have a thousand feathers."

Becka turned to see a tall brave wearing a full headdress made of bright red feathers from head to toe. "Wow!" she exclaimed. "He looks awesome."

Scott nodded. "But he must have wiped out the entire cardinal population from here to the Arizona state line."

"Those aren't cardinal feathers." Rebecca almost laughed. "They dye the feathers to get them that color."

"Oh yeah," Scott said, obviously trying to cover his ignorance. "I knew that."

Becka smiled.

"But the thing that really gets me is—"

"Shh," she said, "Swift Arrow is talking again. Listen."

They directed their attention back to the clearing where Swift Arrow stood on a tree stump, trying to explain Christianity to his people. "You need not be afraid of angry gods," he was saying. "There is only one God, and he is a loving God. The Father of us all."

There was a quiet buzz among the people. Swift Arrow continued, "The evil in the world comes from the devil. But he is not all-powerful. He is only a fallen angel. You do not have to make sacrifices to him for protection. All you have to do is believe in God's Son, Jesus Christ. He came down from heaven to die for what we have done wrong. He came to suffer and take the punishment for our sins. We need only believe in him and ask him to be our chief, our Lord. We need only obey him and accept his free gift of salvation in order that we might have ever-lasting peace with our Father."

"What of the teachings of our ancestors?" a tall brave with three feathers in his hair demanded.

"It is as you've always suspected," Swift Arrow answered. "Some of it is true, and some of it is false. Dark Bear has twisted the teachings to suit himself. He is keeping you from the real truth."

Scott leaned over to Becka and whispered, "He preaches a pretty good sermon."

Becka nodded as she searched the crowd.

"Who are you looking for?" Scott asked.

"Dark Bear. I was hoping he'd at least drop by for a listen."

"Or a major showdown," Scott added.

"Well, even that might have been OK. But if he's not here, where is he? What is he up to?"

~

Not far away, at the site of the avalanche and Dark Bear's holy place, a small fire burned. And Dark Bear danced around that fire furiously. He paused only for a moment, just long enough to throw an angry look back toward Swift Arrow's council. And then, ever so slowly, he reached into the satchel hanging around his neck. He pulled out a handful of fine, blue powder, then tossed it into the fire.

There was a loud whoosh as flames shot high into the sky, then immediately died down. Once again, Dark Bear lowered his head and began dancing . . . and chanting. . . .

~

"Jesus Christ is not the white man's God." Swift Arrow continued speaking to the crowd, and some were beginning to listen. "He is everyone's God. He was born a Jew and lived and died in Palestine two thousand years ago—nearly fifteen hundred years before the white man came and drove us from our land. The white man has embraced his truth, yes, but so have millions of Chinese, Africans, Latin Americans, and people all over the world. The God of the Bible is not the God of the white man. He is the God of *all* people."

There was a loud crack of thunder. Instinctively, Swift Arrow turned toward Dark Bear's holy place. In the distance, he could see the reflection of a fire as it burned. Against the cliffs, he could make out the flickering of a shadow . . . the shadow of a man dancing.

Swift Arrow forced himself to continue. "It is not my fault that the rain has not come. It is not a punishment from the gods. Dark Bear has misled you."

A handful of people nodded their heads in agreement. A few coughed lightly. It was soft at first, but the coughing grew until it was obvious someone was starting to choke.

~

Becka tensed. It was the same choking Scotty had experienced earlier. Now others were starting to cough and gasp for breath.

Rebecca threw a look to Scott. This was not good. Not good at all. One, two, a handful of people dropped to their knees, coughing, choking, and struggling to breathe. And to make matters worse, they were the very ones who had been nodding their heads in agreement. "Dark Bear," Rebecca whispered.

Scott nodded. "We'd better do something fast."

"Like what? What can we do?"

"Satan," Scott spoke softly, "in the name of Jesus Christ, we command you to stop this coughing."

"That's right," Becka whispered in agreement. "In the name of Christ, we demand that you stop this attack."

Scott nodded. "Whatever evil is at work here, we remind you that the name of Jesus is stronger than any other name, and it is by his name that we order you to leave and command that peace and health be restored back to these people. Now. We command you to leave now!"

Immediately, the coughing subsided. While a few people remained on the ground, trying to recover their wits, others rose and began to breathe normally. Most, however, were simply anxious to leave. They knew what had happened, and they wanted no more of it. They started moving, shoving, and trying to get as far away from Swift Arrow's council as possible.

Swift Arrow watched helplessly as his people left the clearing and headed for their homes. He looked broken and defeated. His council was over. And if anything had been proven, it was that Dark Bear's strength and influence were more powerful than his own.

8

Before going to
bed that night, Rebecca and Scott offered to
pray with Swift Arrow. He was clearly
defeated, and they wanted to encourage him.

"Listen," Rebecca told him, "when things
get the toughest, that's when God works his
greatest miracles."

"That's right," Scott agreed. "When we're
our weakest, that's when he's the strongest."

Swift Arrow nodded, but it was obvious his heart was anything but encouraged. He had finally worked up the courage to face Dark Bear, and all he had been met with was defeat.

"Dear Lord," Becka prayed as they bowed their heads together, "we know you shine brightest in the darkest places. And right now, at least on the surface, everything looks bad. We ask—we pray in Jesus' name—that you step in now. That you take what our enemy has chosen for evil and turn it around for good. We ask this because of your great love for us and for this whole village. We ask this in your Son's precious and holy name. Amen."

Scott and Swift Arrow joined in the amen. Then, before they headed off to bed, all three agreed to pray again first thing in the morning. Becka could see that that gave Swift Arrow some assurance, but she was still concerned. About Ryan.

She hadn't seen him all day, and her worries had only increased. She chose to wait up for him. It was nearly ten o'clock when he finally lumbered into camp. He looked very tired, and there was a strangely distant look in his eyes.

"We missed you tonight," Rebecca said as he approached, heading for his tent.

He slowed to a stop but said nothing.

She tried again. "You would have really loved the council. Swift Arrow made a great speech, and you should have seen all the people dressed in their outfits."

"Ceremonial clothes," Ryan corrected her.

"Right, ceremonial clothes. It was great." She waited for him to say something else, but when he didn't, she finally asked, "Where were you?"

"Off with Little Creek. He's teaching me a lot of stuff."

It was Rebecca's turn to remain quiet. The silence grew.

"Listen," Ryan finally said, "I'm sorry I haven't been around very much lately, but I'm really trying to make the most of this trip."

"Sure . . . I understand." It was a lie. Becka didn't understand. By 'making the most of this trip, did he mean staying away from her? Was he saying he wanted to cool off their relationship? Or was it something else? Was it more about God than about her? There was so much she wanted to ask Ryan. Maybe another moonlight stroll on the ridge would help. Maybe there he could finally open up and share what he was feeling. She was just about to suggest it when he turned abruptly and started for his tent.

"Ryan . . ."

He turned back toward her. "What?"

But the words would not come. She shrugged. "Nothing."

He started to turn, but she had to say something.

"Just . . . we could sure use your support tomorrow. Dark Bear did a real number at Swift Arrow's council tonight. People were choking and gasping for air and everything. And tomorrow night is Dark Bear's council. So we're going to get together first thing in the morning and pray with Swift Arrow."

Ryan nodded absently. "I'll try to be there. Listen, it's getting pretty late. . . ."

Becka shrugged. "Of course, back home we'd consider this too early to go to bed."

"Yeah," Ryan answered, "but things are a lot different here than back home."

Becka nodded. They certainly were.

"Well . . . good night." And then, without another word, he stooped down and disappeared into his tent.

Becka sat there trying to swallow back the tightness growing in her throat. Maybe it really was over between them. Maybe he really did want to call it quits. She closed her eyes. Actually, that would be good news compared to her other fear. The fear that something was coming between Ryan and God.

"'In the last times some will turn away from what we believe,'" Z had quoted. "'They will follow lying spirits and teachings that come from demons.'"

She took a deep breath and let it out. She knew whom Z was talking about. Something was happening to Ryan. Something spiritual. And something very, very evil . . .

Aaaooowlll . . .

The wind blew strongly that night. It howled through the canyon, making it impossible for Ryan to sleep. He lay awake, his mind running in a thousand directions at once. What he'd experienced in the cave . . . was that really the Great Spirit choosing him? And was the Great Spirit really God, the same God he had learned to follow and love as a Christian? But if it was the same God, why did he feel so uneasy? And yet why was he so attracted to it, so anxious to go deeper, to connect more fully with it, with this . . . spirit?

Aaaooowlll . . .

Scott bolted up in his sleeping bag, even though he looked like he was still half-asleep. "What was that?" he mumbled.

"I think it's the wind," Ryan said.

"I don't know," Scott muttered. "I was dreaming about a wolf. Maybe it's a wolf."

Aaaooowlll . . .

"Whatever it is, it's down in the canyon," Ryan said. "Maybe it's Dark Bear. Little Creek says some of the old shamans could change themselves into animals—usually wolves or bears. They call it . . . shape-shifting."

Scott didn't answer, and Ryan realized he had already drifted back to sleep.

Aaaooowlll . . .

Ryan knew it was no wolf. But he also knew it was more than the wind. There was something inside it, something calling. Something connected to the eagle. Something calling him . . .

Unable to sleep and growing more and more attracted to the sound, Ryan quietly crawled from his sleeping bag, slipped on his clothes, and stepped out into the night.

It was exhilarating. The stars. The full moon. The wind. He'd barely stepped out of the tent, drinking it all in, when the cry came again.

Aaaooowlll . . .

For the briefest second, he thought it was Little Creek signaling him. But this was something far deeper and more important. He sensed that it was somehow connected to the

Great Spirit. Feeling the pull more strongly, he finally gave in to the impulse. He began walking toward Dark Bear's holy place.

Ever since the avalanche, he had wanted to go back to the place of stones. And since the encounter with the eagle in the cave, the desire had become irresistible.

As he walked, Ryan reached into his jacket pocket. The flask Little Creek had given him was still there. Ryan knew he had another choice awaiting him. He could continue being what he now thought was a coward— he could continue going only halfway, being caught between the two worlds and never finding out the truth. Or he could have the courage to go all the way, to see what was really out there, to totally give in and see what the Great Spirit really had in store.

With a deep breath, he chose the latter. He shook the flask, making sure there was still plenty of tea left. He unscrewed the lid. The warning bells went off again, but this time they were faint, barely discernible. Still, just to be certain, he lifted the flask to his lips and quickly drank down the tea before he could change his mind.

There . . . now he'd done it. In just a few minutes, it would begin.

It wasn't long before the canyon began to shift and move, almost like it was a living organism. The wind continued its howling, but now he could hear the voices clearly. Human voices. By the time he arrived at the place of stones, the tea's effect was incredible. Ryan looked up. There, just as he had expected, perched on the highest rock, was the magnificent eagle.

It sat there majestically, looking at him, waiting for him. And then, a moment later, it spread out its giant wings.

Instinctively Ryan extended his own arms as if he, too, had wings.

Then they were flying. Together. Soaring over the great peaks and canyons, taking turns diving into the valley. Circling higher and higher and higher.

And then Ryan slept.

~

Rebecca was up at dawn. She dressed and headed for the boys' tent. This was the morning of prayer, when they would join together and intercede for Swift Arrow, against Dark Bear. This was when the job would really be done. But when Becka got to the tent and pushed open the flap, Ryan was gone.

"Scott!" she called. She reached in and shook him. "Scotty, wake up!"

"Wha-what?"

"Where's Ryan?" she demanded. "Where did Ryan go?"

Scott roused himself a bit and looked over at Ryan's sleeping bag. "He's . . . Where'd he go?" Scott frowned, trying to remember. "The wolf."

"What are you talking about?"

"He left last night." Scott reached for his shirt. "Give me a sec', and I'll help you look for him."

A minute later the two were off looking for Ryan.

"What were you saying about wolves?" Rebecca asked.

"I don't remember. I mean, it sounded like a wolf."

"There was a wolf out here?" Becka cried in alarm. "You let him go out and see if there was a wolf?"

Scott frowned and rubbed his head. "No . . . that was the dream part. At least, I think it was a dream. But I do remember the wind howling and him getting up in the middle of the night."

"We've got to find him," Becka said. "Something's wrong; I know it."

But they didn't find him. The two looked everywhere in the village but with no success. And since they didn't see Little Creek, they assumed he and Ryan were together.

"I think we need to talk to Z again," Rebecca finally said. "That Bible verse he gave us—I'm pretty sure I understand it now."

"You do?"

"I think part of it is a warning for Ryan."

"Let me head back to the tent and get my laptop," Scott said. "I'll meet you at the general store in five minutes."

Rebecca agreed, and in less than half that amount of time, they were again connecting the computer to the store's phone outlet.

When Scott logged in, Z was not there, but his answer was already waiting:

Remember, you are fighting two battles . . . one offense, the other defense. Regardless of the fight, your weapons are the same: prayer and the Word of God. Activate these weapons through faith. If you do, you will be victorious. If you do not, you will perish. Z

Ryan woke up in the cave. He wasn't sure how he'd gotten there until he saw Little Creek by the dim light of the lantern.

"Hello," Little Creek said. "I found you asleep on top of the stones in Dark Bear's holy place. I couldn't rouse you, and I was afraid you'd be blistered by the sun, so I dragged you in here."

"I'm in the cave *again?*" Ryan groaned.

Little Creek smiled. "Yeah. If I'm to be your personal taxi and haul you from place to place, I'll have to start charging a fare."

Ryan smiled, and Little Creek asked, "You took the tea again, didn't you?"

Ryan slowly sat up, then looked deep into his friend's eyes. "I flew with the eagle."

"No!" Little Creek cried in astonishment. "Really?"

Ryan nodded.

"You flew with the eagle? I only know one other who has done such a thing. What was it like?"

"It was . . . " Ryan paused, remembering. And then he grinned. "Incredible."

∿

When Rebecca and Scott returned to their tent, they found Swift Arrow already waiting with their mom.

"Before we start our prayer," Swift Arrow said quietly, "I must say I'm not even certain I have heard correctly from the Lord."

"What do you mean?" Mom asked gently.

Swift Arrow frowned. "How do I even know this is what the Lord wants?"

"Swift Arrow," Becka began, "we just got

off the Internet with Z. He says we have two tools, the Bible and prayer. You know the Word; you know God wants to reach your village with his love. He wants to reach everybody."

Swift Arrow looked down and nodded. "I know God wants the people of Starved Rock to be saved. But perhaps . . . I'm not the man to do it. I am too timid, too weak."

"No way," Scott protested. "David was just a punk kid when God used him against Goliath. He was weak, but he was strong because his strength depended upon God."

Swift Arrow nodded. "But David was a man of great faith."

"What about Moses?" Mom added. "He had so little faith he didn't want the job God asked him to do. Or Jonah. He tried to get out of what God had called him for. The Bible couldn't be clearer, Swift Arrow. God uses whom ~~he~~ chooses. It doesn't have to make sense to us, just to God. All you have to do is be willing to obey."

Swift Arrow looked at the three of them. "I guess I'd better start agreeing with you or you will never stop preaching at me. Am I correct?"

Scott and Becka both broke out laughing. Mom grinned along with them.

"You got that right," Scott agreed.

"Just tell us you'll obey God's Word and not give up," Becka said.

Swift Arrow almost smiled. "All right, all right. I will obey. I will not give up."

"That's all it takes," Mom said.

"But what should I do?"

"Follow Z's advice," Becka said. "We know what the Word of God says about this situation. Now all that is left is to pray."

"May we begin?" Swift Arrow asked.

"Let's do it," Scott said.

And so the four began to pray. . . . At first they started off with quiet worshiping, thanking God for his past faithfulness. Then they sang a couple worship songs that they all knew. And finally, they began thanking the Lord in advance for what he was about to do. They weren't sure what the details would be, but they were sure of one thing: It would be awesome. It always was when God did something.

But even as they prayed, even as they prepared for whatever that night would bring, Becka could not shake the nagging feeling in the back of her mind.

Ryan was in danger.

9

It was nearly lunchtime when Ryan returned to camp. Rebecca was lighting the grill to cook hot dogs. When she saw Ryan and Little Creek, she leaped to her feet and raced to Ryan.

"Where have you been? I've been worried about you. . . . Where did you go?"

Ryan threw her a glance. For the first time

she could remember, he looked irritated with her. "I just went out, OK? Your brother thought he heard a noise, and I went out to investigate."

"What did you find?"

He looked at her strangely. "Where?"

"When you went out to investigate. What did you find?"

Ryan shrugged. "Nothing."

"Then why didn't you come back? Why weren't you here for prayer with Swift Arrow, like you said you would be?"

Finally Ryan exploded. "Will you stop trying to own me!"

A moment of silence followed. Part of Rebecca wanted to turn and run away, but there was something wrong here, and she had to get to the bottom of it. When she answered, she was surprised at how calm and controlled her voice sounded. "I just asked where you were."

"I was busy," he snapped.

Becka stood, unsure what to do. She was grateful when Mom, always the peacekeeper, called out from her place near the grill, "Ryan . . . are you guys hungry? We've got plenty of hot dogs here. What about you, Little Creek? You must be starved."

"Thanks," Ryan said softly. "I'm famished."

"Me too," Little Creek added.

After lunch Mom headed back to the store for some groceries and Scotty and Little Creek decided to gather up firewood for the evening. That left Rebecca sitting by herself, staring off into the mountains.

"Beautiful, aren't they?" Ryan said softly from behind her.

Becka sighed. "Yeah, I suppose."

"You suppose?" he asked as he crossed to the log and joined her.

She gave no answer.

"Look," Ryan began, "I know I let you down this morning."

Becka said nothing.

"But the reason we're out here is for spiritual stuff, isn't it? I'm just trying to learn all these cool things God is showing me."

Rebecca looked at him, meeting his eyes for the first time. "How do you know that?"

"How do I know it's cool? Because Little Creek has been—"

"No," Rebecca interrupted. "How do you know *God* is showing you these things?"

Ryan shook his head. "Don't be afraid of stuff just because it's different, Beck."

"I'm not afraid, but I'm not taking dangerous chances either."

"Who's taking chances?" There was no

missing the edge in Ryan's voice. "I'm just learning about another culture."

"By trying out all its rituals?" Becka asked. "After all we've been through, that sounds pretty risky to me."

Ryan looked away. She'd hit a nerve, and she knew it.

Suddenly he was on his feet. "I knew you'd take it this way," he muttered angrily. "I was hoping to be able to share with you some of the wonderful experiences I've been having, but of course you're judging me before I can get a word out."

He started walking away, but now Rebecca was on her feet. "Then why don't you tell me?" He stopped, and she continued, "You're right, Ryan. I am being judgmental, but it's because I don't know anything you've been doing. I mean, what do you and Little Creek do out there all day? Where do you go?"

Before Ryan could answer, Scott and Little Creek appeared, each carrying an armload of firewood.

"Hey, guys," Scott said. "What's up?"

"Your sister," Ryan grumbled. "As usual, she's up in her ivory tower trying to tell the rest of us what to do."

Becka bit her lip. She felt hot tears spring

to her eyes, but she would not let Ryan see her cry. Not now. Not here.

Ryan spun around and headed back out, away from camp. Little Creek dumped his load of firewood and started after him. "Hey, Ryan! Ryan, wait up."

A long moment of silence followed. Now the tears were spilling onto Becka's cheeks. But that was OK because now there was nobody to see them.

"Hey, Beck . . ." Nobody but Scotty. "Becka, you all right?"

She nodded without looking at him. "Yeah." Her voice was hoarse with emotion. "Yeah, I'm OK."

"Did you find out what's eating him?"

Rebecca shook her head.

He sighed loudly. "That's too bad." Then he turned and walked away.

Becka was grateful that Scotty was leaving because she had made up her mind. If Ryan wouldn't tell her what he was up to, she would find out for herself.

✳

It wasn't difficult to follow Ryan and Little Creek out of the village and into the mountains. Knowing Little Creek's keen senses, Becka gave the boys plenty of leeway so they wouldn't see or hear her. Soon they arrived

at what she took to be Dark Bear's holy
place. It fit what they'd described . . . and it
gave her the creeps. The ground was still covered from the avalanche. She looked at the
stones and frowned. There was a pattern in
the way they lay on the ground.

Dark Bear had been hard at work.

Just then Little Creek and Ryan veered off
the path and headed into the weeds. Rebecca
followed. The brush and grass were up to her
chest, and it was hard not to lose track of the
guys while trying to walk as quietly as possible.

They were approaching a tall, looming
cliff. The ground sloped steeply, and it was a
struggle to keep her footing as she followed
them. Eventually they came to the base of
the cliff. At the bottom was a round, dark
shadow . . . a cave.

Crouching low in the weeds, Rebecca
watched Ryan and Little Creek enter the
cave. She wondered how far it went, if she
could follow them in without being spotted—or getting lost. It was worth the risk.
She silently crossed to the cave, took a look
inside, and then entered.

It was entirely dark inside, except for the
reflection of Little Creek's light up ahead.
Carefully, Rebecca inched her way along the
cave floor, trying to keep quiet and yet trying to keep the light in view. But she could

not do both. The light was moving too quickly. For one brief moment she wanted to run back to the entrance before she was plunged into total darkness, but she fought off the impulse. She'd come this far, and she wasn't about to back down now.

She glanced back toward the dim light. To her relief, it no longer seemed to be moving. The guys must have stopped. She scurried along, trying to be as quiet as possible. She eased forward little by little until, finally, she saw them.

Ryan and Little Creek were building a fire in the middle of a large, open cavern. The flames came to life, lighting the cavern and creating dancing shadows on the walls. Becka watched as Little Creek took a small flask out of his bag and handed it to Ryan. "Are you sure you want to take it again so close to the last time?"

Ryan nodded and silently reached for the flask. He unscrewed the lid, tilted his head back, and drank. When he was finished, he handed the flask to Little Creek and asked, "Will you stay?"

The Indian shook his head. "It is your time," he said almost reverently. "I will go, but I will leave the light."

Ryan gave a single nod. "Thank you, my brother."

Little Creek turned and headed back out of the cavern, toward Rebecca. She pressed herself flat against the opposite wall as the boy approached. Without a light, she knew it would be difficult for him to see her. As long as she remained low and quiet, he would pass and she would remain unnoticed. She held her breath as he moved past her.

It seemed like minutes before she could no longer hear his steps. Then, ever so carefully, she eased back around the corner. Ryan now stood in the center of the large cavern. He was looking intently at a wall about ten feet away. From what she could see of his expression, she had the terrible feeling that whatever he'd drunk was some sort of drug . . . and that it had already started to take effect. He was staring at the wall as if he were seeing something, but there was nothing there.

Or was there?

For the briefest second she thought she saw movement. It was up above, more toward the center of the cavern. She caught the flicker of something . . . a shadow. It disappeared as quickly as it had appeared, but there was no mistaking its form. It appeared to be a giant eagle.

She saw it again, longer this time. It was a misty apparition, half-solid, half-transparent. Becka gasped, and a chill of dread swept over her. It was the eagle from her dreams. Her heart began to pound as she watched it circle above the cavern.

Then she noticed something even more frightening: the crevices and cracks of the cavern's ceiling formed a pattern—the same pattern she had seen covering the sky in her dreams! The lines, triangles, and squares were arranged in the same swirling, concentric design.

Then, just as in her dream, the eagle's harsh cry rang out. She watched in terror as the ghost bird hovered one last moment before beginning its dive.

It was headed directly for Ryan!

"Ryan!" Her cry echoed through the cavern. "Ryan, look out!" He turned toward her—not much, but enough to save him from the bird's talons, which flew past, missing his face by inches.

Becka was on her feet, running toward him. "Ryan! Run, Ryan! Get out of here!"

He stared at her, his face full of confusion, as though he didn't know who she was, why she was there.

The eagle rose toward the ceiling, preparing for another assault. Once again Becka noted how translucent it was—there and yet *not* there. But she had little time to ponder this as it turned and began another dive.

She wouldn't reach Ryan, not in time. All she could do was pray. "Be gone, dark spirit!" she shouted. "You have no power over a servant of Christ!"

At the mention of Christ's name, the eagle shrieked.

Rebecca watched in astonishment as the bird suddenly changed shape. The eagle's sleek and elegant form mutated before her eyes. Its wings remained, but the colorful feathers turned to crusty, black leather. At the same time, the creature's legs grew to thick, stubby knobs and its talons grew longer—sharper and more deadly.

But the greatest change was the bird's head. The smooth crown rippled into craggy bone and flesh, taking on a hideous appearance that was part toad, part gargoyle.

Instantly Becka recognized it. She'd seen its kind before, on more than one occasion. And although she felt a cold shiver ripple down her spine, she knew what to do.

She planted her feet firmly and shouted, "Demon of hell, in the name of Jesus Christ, I command you to leave this place!"

Ryan stood watching, unable to move. He felt as if he were in a dream. He knew what was happening, but he couldn't react. All he could do was stare at Becka as she took her stand. But then, behind her, he saw something else. Another movement.

Dark Bear had entered the cavern.

Ryan wanted to yell, to warn her, but the drug wouldn't allow him to speak. He watched in terror as Dark Bear crept up behind Rebecca and raised his staff. Desperately Ryan tried to move his mouth, his lips, anything to make a noise, to warn her. But no sound would come.

He watched helplessly as Dark Bear brought the staff down hard onto Rebecca's head. She slumped to the floor, unconscious. Ryan continued to stare as the shaman picked Becka up and carried her back toward an area of the cavern he had never explored. Again Ryan tried to cry out, to move, but again he could make no sound. He could make no movement. Now the cave was starting to spin, to twirl. It began to rotate, starting to fly. Hit by a wave of nausea, Ryan dropped to his knees. He convulsed once, twice, before throwing up. He looked up and caught one final glimpse of Becka. Still in Dark Bear's arms, still being carried off to her death.

And still he could not move. A moment later, he passed out.

10

When Ryan
awoke, the effects of the drug had not
entirely worn off. His head was still spinning,
and the first time he tried to stand, he fell
back to the ground. He got up again more
slowly—much more slowly—as memories
flooded in.

Becka! I have to find Rebecca.

With great difficulty, he staggered to the wall where he'd seen Dark Bear carry her. It was solid rock. Had it been another hallucination? He wasn't sure. Carefully, he felt for an opening, a crack. There was nothing.

Without warning his head started to spin. His stomach contracted as nausea again overwhelmed him. He felt awful. But even though his body was weak, his mind continued to race with both fear and regret. If he hadn't taken the tea, he could have saved Rebecca.

Why did he do it? He knew it was stupid to take drugs. And wrong. He'd even studied this kind of thing. The Bible referred to it as *pharmakeia*. . . . It was a sin similar to witchcraft. And wasn't that exactly why he had taken it—to get in touch with the mystical? to experience the supernatural? Ryan let out a painful groan. Why hadn't he seen it earlier? That's exactly what he was doing . . . practicing a form of witchcraft.

"Dear God," he whispered hoarsely. "I'm sorry. I'm so sorry. . . . Please forgive me. I'll never do that again, I promise. I'm so sorry. Please, help me find Becka. . . . Help me to help her. Please . . ."

A strong sense of calm came over him, as though someone had put an arm around his shoulders. Well, he reasoned, Someone had.

He didn't feel any better, but he knew he was forgiven. Gratitude filled him for God's readiness to forgive. No matter how badly he messed up, all it took was asking forgiveness and being serious about not doing it again. It was as simple as that.

Of course, there were still the consequences of his actions. They had to be faced. Once again he searched for an opening, for some crevice, for anything. And once again nausea overtook him and he fell.

But this time as he struggled to his feet, Ryan reached out to the wall and felt something. A lever. Embedded in the wall. He pulled it. Nothing happened. Then he pushed it.

Suddenly the wall began to move. Ryan staggered back and watched as the large stone rolled to the side. Behind it was a small room, a chamber. And lying on the ground directly in the middle of that chamber, tied and gagged, was Rebecca.

"Becka?" His voice was raspy and dry. "Rebecca?" There was no answer. He stumbled toward her. As he approached, he noticed that the ground was moving again. At first he thought it was the drug, but as he forced his eyes to focus, he saw that it wasn't the cave floor that was moving . . . it was something on the floor. Hundreds of somethings. Brown and orange. And they were huge. Insects? No. His blood ran cold. Not insects.

Scorpions.

∿

Back at camp, Mom, Scott, and Swift Arrow were beginning to worry about Becka and Ryan. Dark Bear's council would take place in just a few hours, and the two were nowhere to be found. In fact, nobody had seen them since lunch.

"That's not like Rebecca," Mom said. "She always lets us know where she's going."

"Let's walk through the village," Swift Arrow suggested. "Perhaps she is trying to talk to the people about tonight."

Scott agreed to accompany him, and the two began their search. A few minutes later, Swift Arrow asked, "Do you see how the people avert their eyes from me?"

Scott nodded. "After last night, they're all afraid of Dark Bear."

"It looks as though they have already made their choice. Perhaps I was not the man to bring the gospel here."

Scott shook his head. "Don't be discouraged, Swift Arrow. You still have tonight."

"I know, and yet . . ."

"And yet what?"

"I can only take the news that your sister and Ryan are missing as another sign favoring Dark Bear."

Scott nodded. "Maybe. But there's a saying in baseball that applies to exactly the type of warfare we're involved in."

"What's that?" Swift Arrow asked.

"It ain't over till it's over."

∿

Ryan had pulled a big stick from the fire and was doing his best to keep the scorpions away from Becka. But no matter how many he swiped away, more continued to come.

It wasn't long before Becka began to stir. When she opened her eyes, she blinked, as though trying to focus. She looked at Ryan, then at what he was doing, and then she rubbed her face against a rock until she was able to finally push the gag from her mouth.

"Ryan!" she said with a cough. "Listen to me. . . . We've—we've got to pray."

"I *am* praying!" Ryan shouted back, smashing the stick down on the head of another scorpion.

Becka went on as though he hadn't spoken. "I know you didn't mean to, but you've formed some kind of allegiance to Dark Bear . . . through all these rituals you've been doing. You've got to renounce it, Ryan.

You've got to break his magic's power over you."

Ryan's head still swam from the effects of the drug as he swatted at the scorpions. "What about these—"

"These what?"

"These scorpions!"

Becka lifted her head and narrowed her eyes, as though straining to see. "Ryan, there are no scorpions here."

"What are you talking about?" Was she nuts? They were everywhere!

"There's nothing here," she repeated firmly. "It's more of Dark Bear's magic."

"But . . ." He hesitated. Was it possible? Could she be right?

"Pray," Becka urged. "You've got to pray and break your allegiance to Dark Bear."

Ryan watched a particularly nasty scorpion turn and head directly for Becka, directly for her face.

"Pray, Ryan. Pray!"

It was nearly there, approaching her cheek.

"Pray!"

He cried out desperately, "Lord! Lord, forgive me. In the name of Jesus, I break any allegiances I've formed with demonic powers. I break the power of Dark Bear's magic."

Just like that, the scorpion was gone. They were all gone.

Ryan blinked his eyes, trying to take it in. "You're right!" he shouted. "They were an illusion! They're gone. They're all gone."

"Hurry and untie me!" Rebecca cried. "Dark Bear's council is coming up. Swift Arrow is going to need our help. Hurry, Ryan. Hurry!"

~

Back at the village, Dark Bear's council had already begun. He stood next to the crackling fire, addressing the crowd. His eyes were wild with intensity. "There is one here who is a thorn among the flowers, a sharp-edged rock among the smooth. One who speaks against the laws of the ancient ones. One who dares grumble against the god of thunder and lightning. One who has offended the rain god."

Scott stood beside Mom at the back of the crowd. He glanced over at Swift Arrow, who was growing more tense with Dark Bear's every word. In fact, even from this distance, Scott could see him starting to tremble. Not that Scott blamed him. Dark Bear was more than a little menacing. With his warrior clothes, his bright feathers and buffalo-horn headdress, the shaman looked invincible. It was clear that the people feared him. But more terrifying than his appearance was the confidence with which he spoke: "Swift Arrow is the reason there has been no rain!"

Some of the people began to grumble in agreement.

"Swift Arrow has angered the rain god with his white man's lies! There will be no rain until he has been driven from the tribe!"

Scott glanced over at Swift Arrow, and their eyes met. It was now or never. Taking his cue, Swift Arrow stepped forward. "That's not true! My tribesmen, the drought began long before I returned to the village. You know that. And I have spoken the truth to you. Jesus is not the white man's God. He is the Son of the one true God. Of everybody's God. And if you will but—"

"Silence!" Dark Bear bellowed. "If we let him speak these lies, rain will never fall upon our ground! Even his white friends have deserted him because they know he lies."

More people started to mumble in agreement. By now everyone in the village knew of Ryan and Rebecca's disappearance.

It was obvious that this threw Swift Arrow, but he did not back down. "My friends have not deserted me!"

"Then where have they gone?" Dark Bear demanded.

"Look!" He pointed toward Scott and

Mom. "Here is the girl's mother. Here is her brother. They have not deserted me. They fear something has happened to the girl and the boy to keep them from being here as well."

Dark Bear took a menacing step closer to Swift Arrow. His voice grew low and vehement. "If something has happened to them, then it is the gods themselves who have taken vengeance."

The declaration almost sent Swift Arrow staggering, but Dark Bear wasn't done. He raised his voice so all could hear. "I warned them not to ally with you, but they would not listen. Instead, they followed your lies, and now they have paid the price."

Suddenly a strong voice shot through the clearing. "It is *you* who lie, Dark Bear."

Rebecca!

Scott spun around to see her and Ryan approaching.

"Thank you, Lord," he heard Mom pray quietly beside him.

Becka continued, "You lied to your own tribe, Dark Bear. Just now, I heard you. I did not leave Swift Arrow's side. You kidnapped me!"

The tribe murmured.

Becka shouted over them. "You kidnapped me and left me tied up in your cave.

You are a *liar.* Like your father, the devil, you are the author of—"

Scott was the first to see it. "Look out!"

The eagle came in so fast that Rebecca barely had time to duck. It was huge, bigger than any eagle Scott had ever seen. But it was more than an eagle. As it soared back into the sky, preparing for another attack, Scott could actually see stars through its semitransparent wings. No, this was no eagle. It was something far more dangerous. Something he had run into on more than one occasion.

Other people saw it too. They began to race for cover, scrambling for protection. But Rebecca stood her ground. "Be gone, you spirit of hell!"

The creature continued its course. When it reached the height of its circle, it turned and began to dive . . . directly for her.

It was a test. A challenge of Becka's faith, to see if she would back down. For a moment she hesitated, unsure if she could continue. Scott saw her fear and broke toward her. But Ryan was already there, stepping up beside her. Now the creature was bearing down toward them both.

"You fooled me once," Ryan shouted, "but not again!"

It continued to dive, but Ryan and Becka remained firm, unflinching.

"You have no authority!" Ryan shouted. "Your power has already been defeated."

It was nearly on top of them, its talons extended, its beak open wide.

Now it was Becka's turn. "By the power and blood of Jesus Christ, we command you to show your true self!"

The talons were within feet of their faces.

"Now!" Ryan shouted. "Reveal yourself *now!*"

Suddenly the bird veered off, coming so close that wind from its wings blew their hair. But Becka and Ryan didn't budge as the creature swooped upward. Now its movements were sharp, jerky—as though it was struggling with some unseen force. Then there was a flash of light . . . and in place of the eagle was the hideous form of a demon.

The villagers shouted and screamed as the reptilian creature was exposed for all to see.

It circled one last time, preparing for the final assault, but by now three other people had joined Becka and Ryan: Scott, Mom, and Swift Arrow.

It started toward them, its wings drawn together as it began screaming through the air. Now it was Swift Arrow who shouted. His voice rang with clear and absolute authority.

"Spirit of hell, I order you to be gone! You have no power here. In the name of Jesus Christ, we cast you into the pit of hell!"

There was another burst of light, much brighter than the first. With the flash came a pounding clap of thunder. And when everyone's eyes readjusted to the darkness, there was no creature to be found. It was gone. Completely.

Some of the crowd emerged from their places of safety, staring up at the sky—then looking at Swift Arrow and marveling at his authority.

But the confrontation wasn't completely over. Not yet.

Dark Bear raised his staff high into the air and shouted, "Swift Arrow, you must die! You and your friends, you all must die!" He spread his arms to the sky and called, "God of the lightning, god of thunder, I beseech you, show these people. Show them once and for all who has the power. Show them who has the authority!"

Suddenly, a great bolt of lightning flashed out of the darkness. It forked through the sky directly toward the gathering. Before anyone had a chance to run or duck, it struck. But it did not strike the crowd. Nor did it strike Swift Arrow and his friends. Instead, it forked sharply to the side and hit Dark Bear, knocking him to the ground.

Everyone stared in astonishment. The man was still breathing, but no one dared approach. No one but Swift Arrow. He started toward him, and as he knelt by Dark Bear's side, Scott heard him speak clearly and with compassion. "The Lord will no longer allow you to use your power for evil, Dark Bear."

Dark Bear opened his eyes but remained motionless.

Swift Arrow continued, "He has spared your life, but God has proven his power. Your strength has been broken, and now our people can see the truth."

He gently reached down to the shaman, helping him sit up—and a most remarkable thing began to happen. Ryan was the first to feel it. Something wet and cold on his arm. A drop. And then another . . . and another.

"It's starting to rain!" he shouted.

Becka and Mom looked up. It was true. This time the thunder and lightning had finally brought the rain. And it came down faster and harder with each passing minute.

None of the villagers ran for cover this time. Instead, they tilted back their heads. Some opened their mouths. Others were shouting and starting to laugh. Scott laughed, too, with relief. With gratitude. Dark Bear's curse had been broken. Swift Arrow's God had shown his power . . . and his compassion. Now the villagers knew the truth. It would be up to each of them to decide whether or not to follow it.

But at least they knew the truth.

~

It was still raining as the group packed to leave the following morning.

"Where is Dark Bear?" Scott asked as he adjusted his backpack and prepared to begin the descent into the valley.

"Dark Bear fled earlier this morning," Swift Arrow explained. "The tribe will soon appoint his replacement."

"I have a sneaking suspicion who that person will be." Becka grinned.

Swift Arrow shrugged and smiled. "That will be up to the Lord. But this time the leader's medicine and his words—" He produced a small pocket Bible—"this time they will be the truth."

The group nodded in agreement. As they prepared to leave, they promised Swift Arrow that they would continue to pray for him and for his village. Hugs were given all around, and promises were made to stay in touch.

"Good-bye, my friends," Swift Arrow said. There was no missing the emotion in his voice. "You have taught me much."

"And you, Swift Arrow," Scott said. "You have taught us a lot too."

And then, after another round of hugs, they were off.

"There's just one other person I wanted to say good-bye to," Ryan said as they made their way through the village.

"Who's that?" Becka asked.

"Ryan! Ryan, wait up."

The group turned to see Little Creek running to catch up with them.

"There you are." Ryan grinned. "I was just saying I was sorry we missed you."

Little Creek grinned and extended his hand. "Good-bye, my friends," he said as he shook each hand. "Good-bye, good-bye, good-bye—" he saved Ryan's hand for last— "and good-bye. I have learned an interesting lesson from you, Ryan."

"What's that?"

"That the teacher should sometimes be the student. I was so anxious to teach you the ways of my tribe that I missed what you had to teach me."

Ryan smiled and nodded. "I understand. But Swift Arrow can teach you those things now."

Little Creek nodded. "I believe he can."

Once again Little Creek insisted on shaking each hand as final good-byes were said. And then, at last, they were heading out of the village.

Thanks to the rain, the day was cooler, and the walk across the plateau proved to be refreshing and uneventful. Even the rope bridge was almost enjoyable.

When they finally arrived at the bottom of the range to their designated pick-up point, Oakey Doakey was there waiting for them in his Jeep, just as he had promised.

"Did you folks have an interesting time?" he asked.

"*Interesting* isn't the word!" Mom exclaimed.

"You got that right," Ryan agreed. "I tell you, I sure learned some valuable lessons."

"I think we all did," Becka said softly.

Ryan nodded and gave her a hug. And, although he didn't see it, she practically beamed in response.

"Hey, what's this?" Scott asked as he climbed into the back.

"What's what?" Mom asked.

"It's a package with our names on it."

"It arrived at my house the day before yesterday," Oakey Doakey said. "I thought I'd bring it up with me. I was particularly intrigued by the return address."

"Where's it from?" Becka asked.

"It really doesn't have an address, just a name."

"A name?"

"Well, not even that," Oakey said. "Just a single letter."

Rebecca and Ryan exchanged looks.

"Kind of curious, really. But does the letter *Z* mean anything to anybody?"

The entire group traded glances with one another. There was no need to speak. Everyone knew exactly what the others had on their minds.

Oh, boy, here we go again. . . .

AUTHOR'S NOTE

As I continue writing this series, I have two equal and opposing concerns. First, I don't want the reader to be too frightened of the devil. Compared to Jesus Christ, Satan is a wimp. The two aren't even in the same league. Although the supernatural evil in these books is based on a certain amount of fact, it's important to understand the awesome protection Jesus Christ offers to all those who have committed their lives to him.

This brings me to my second and somewhat opposing concern: Although the powers of darkness are nothing compared to the power of Jesus Christ and the authority he has given his followers, spiritual warfare is not something we casually stroll into. The situations in these novels are extreme to create suspense and drama. But if you should find yourself involved in something even vaguely similar, don't confront it alone. Find an older, more mature Christian (such as a parent, pastor, or youth leader) to talk to. Ask that person to check out the situation to see what is happening and to help you deal with it.

Yes, we have the victory through Christ, but we should never send in inexperienced soldiers to fight the battle.

Oh, and one final note. When this series was conceived, there were really no bad guys on the Internet. Unfortunately that has changed. Today there are plenty of people out there on the Internet trying to draw young folks into dangerous situations. Although the characters in this series trust Z, if you should run into a similar situation, be smart. Anyone can *sound* kind and understanding, but their intentions may be entirely different. All that to say, don't take candy from strangers you see . . . or trust those you don't.

Bill